Praise for
Mónica Ramón Ríos

"These stylish, often strange stories are like cars on fire themselves—cacophonous, melodious, tragic—and each burn like a symbol of urban resistance. An important and unique contribution to immigrant and protest literature of the Americas."
—Fernando A. Flores, author of *Tears of the Trufflepig*

"Revolution is being waged outside the windows and inside the heads of Mónica Ramón Ríos's characters, obsessed by elsewheres, clawing away the veneer of the everyday. Like a throng of eloquent protestors, electric with rage, these stories occupy a gritty intersection where literature, film, history, and dream cross paths."
—Esther Allen

"*Cars on Fire* describes a prismatic, constellated world in highly chiseled, original prose. This is a book as wise as it is clever, probing, playful, irreverent, original, as it written by an old Kafkan soul in a modern-day, variegated New York, who, with a telling smile and nod to the reader, has acceded to open an ancient portal for a split-second and share a private glimpse of this newly absurd, charged and wispy world in transformation."
—Valerie Miles

MÓNICA
RAMÓN
RÍOS

stories

Translated from the Spanish by Robin Myers

OPEN LETTER
LITERARY TRANSLATIONS FROM THE UNIVERSITY OF ROCHESTER

Library of Congress Cataloging-in-Publication Data: Available.
ISBN-13: 978-1-948830-16-4 | ISBN-10: 1-948830-16-7

This project is supported in part by an award from the National Endowment for the Arts and the New York State Council on the Arts with the support of Governor Andrew M. Cuomo and the New York State Legislature.

Printed on acid-free paper in the United States of America.

Cover design by Jenny Volvovski
Interior design by Anthony Blake

Open Letter is the University of Rochester's nonprofit, literary translation press:
Dewey Hall 1-219, Box 278968, Rochester, NY 14627

www.openletterbooks.org

Contents

CARS
on FIRE

Imprecation

Ramón de Lourdes Ríos Cáceres Solar Benítez Torres de la Parra has endangered our nation. I pray for you, said Our-Lord-Our-God. Berta Teresa Ignacio Montero Montes, you were once a fertile continent, a land replete with natural majesty, a vibrant culture, a spirit humming with vitality and hope. This much was clear, indeed, in the photos our correspondents conveyed to us: your dirty face, your braided hair, your broad smile as you tilled our land, which once belonged to you. Imelda Catalina Rocío Santos del Pilar, you are a great field for us to sow. In you, we ennoble the polis and the police. You are generous, Susana Pedro del Carmen Campos de los Lagos. Today we recognize your dedication to your own metamorphosis. Today we observe you in spike heels, pencil in hand. You speak, Eva María Timoteo de la Cruz Soto Fernández. But it is your very flesh that must speak the people's words and blood.

Ladies, gentlemen, let us hold our mercy close. Our charity is made manifest in your cornfields, in the mines of hunger, in the underground caverns of the world from which Estela Consuelo de Loreto José has emerged. Think benevolently of her on the gallows.

As for me, as a representative of the Presidency and its Headquarters, I'd like to offer a warm Welcome to María

Alonso Rivas de la Rosa so that she may make her speedy Exit from this hall. Jaime Paulina Pedreros de los Mártires de Dios says she traveled skyward and landed here, in our country, seeking to become the grandfather of a family without ever giving birth.

Mariela Fernanda Demetrio Posadas Cerda worked in a coffee shop after she was murdered in Honduras. She served coffee to millionaires after she was murdered in Nicaragua— the very same coffee she planted after she was murdered in Panama, but which ultimately never earned her enough to pay the rent she still owed after she was murdered in Puerto Rico. Guadalupe Mateo de los Ángeles Meza's songrandsonnephew-cousin fell ill as soon as he lost his health insurance after she was murdered in Colombia. And so Ramón de Lourdes Ríos Cáceres Solar Benítez Torres de la Parra came back to life after she contracted an illness and was murdered in Chile.

These are her Words.

Obituary

The Writer

I move in slender fog
but I still wear
the features of my face

. . .

and I answer to my name
although I'm someone else by now.

Gabriela Mistral, "Discovery," *Poem of Chile*

Before the writer died, she'd held long meetings with her lawyers to discuss the possibility of being buried far from her country of origin with all the papers she'd written and never published.

One of the envelopes I'd found on her nightstand, even before I realized that the body in the bed was no longer breathing, contained the signed papers. My name was written on another smaller envelope with the unmistakable green ink she used to draft her manuscripts. Inside it was a long letter dated two days before. It explained why she felt it would do no one any good to read her old notebooks. They'd only find her sorrows, her regrets—not because her life had been dissatisfying, but because her papers were crammed with experiences that had plagued her repeatedly in the form of dreams, night terrors, or when she forgot to take her pills—an empty medicine bottle on her nightstand—even when the people involved were long dead. No one could possibly benefit from reading a compendium of humanity's most hideous features, which had pervaded the writer like fog.

As she once read in a mediocre book—her steady, uniform handwriting informed me that this was how she judged most of her contemporaries—the passing of time was supposed to imply that one had acquired a certain wisdom in focusing on pleasurable things—I could almost hear her say the words, her voice dense with sarcasm. Ever since she was a young woman, she had devoted her mind to resolving matters that any reasonable person would dismiss as unimportant. But they reminded her that there was essentially nothing, deep down, to distinguish her from the gargoyles trapped in limbo between the St. Vitus Cathedral and the rest of Prague. Maybe this was only obvious to me because I'd spent so many years helping the writer with her work and her personal affairs, years in which my own writing was starved of attention, withered by the emotional paroxysms that periodically disfigured her face—the scratch on my left cheek smarted at the sight of her lifeless nails peeking out from under the sheets. It wasn't that she'd killed anyone—with reference to the legal scandal that hounded Mario Vargas Llosa and Rubén Santos Babel—or that she'd destroyed young female writers who wrote like her—an allusion to the article she'd written under a critic's pseudonym for several publications in her home country. What she meant is that she'd let her nightmares ruin every moment of her life, every relationship, every place she'd ever visited—her complaints filled interminable paragraphs. I skimmed them. She hated people, she mistrusted them, and perhaps, the writer mused, her sole raison d'être was to work out their basest inclinations, to fix a clinical eye on everyone who entered her field of vision. Where could this destructive instinct have originated, if she'd had an idyllic childhood and the world rose up sweetly to meet her? Even at a very young age—I remembered the time she'd shoved that academic out of an elevator—she couldn't stand places where people congregate: museums, concerts, parties, gatherings, offices, conferences, readings, houses, living rooms, hallways, public restrooms, and assembly halls. She didn't know how to behave among people she actually knew. She felt more comfortable as the eternal, ever-inaccessible foreigner. This was the source of her countless woes and afflictions, and it explained why she was always on the move.

I thought I heard a sigh leave her body as it lay prone. Out of habit, I got up to check on her, I looked at her face for the first time since I'd entered the room. Her eyes were half-open, her eyelashes metallic. Her skin had taken on the texture of drying wall sealant. Gum, I heard myself say, my voice a wispy thread.

I opened the windows to air out the medicinal smell that had thickened during her dragged-out death throes, however real or imagined her agony may have been. I sat down in an armchair to watch the sun shift along the rug until it reached the foot of the bed and illuminated a delicate curtain of dust spilling down from the books on the nightstand.

Sometime in her thirties, the writer had decided that the only way she could keep on living was to document her regrets in curt, precise, objective sentences. Attaining this literary distance from her own memories, the writer continued, her penmanship listing forward into dramatic peaks, was the only way she could forget. The bookshelves in her house soon filled with notebooks, and the notebooks filled with endlessly repetitive phrases. And so on for decades. The letter piqued my interest at last.

I daydreamed about where the notebooks might be. I knew she'd stashed some of them away in the walls, but what if there were more?

They were nothing but pages and pages of useless drivel—I sensed, in the letter, the writer's desperation to dissuade me from the search, and I felt a rush of pleasure—that no one in their right mind would waste more than an instant thinking about. They overflowed with events that were of little interest to anyone, not even the writer herself, but would soon lodge themselves in her mind like inflection points with hundreds of possible interpretations. Later, much too late, the writer realized things she'd done, emotions she never knew she'd felt. As she stood in the kitchen, knife poised over the butter, or just before bed, or subsumed in a deep sleep, these memories would reappear. Then she'd take out whatever notebook she was keeping at the time.

The sentences soon turned into verses. The verses into songs. The songs into elaborate precepts on the meaning of life, dictates that seeped into her work, the speech of her characters, her narrative style, her own voice. I could almost hear her declare "Tell me what it feels like to be alive"—the edict that would become, thanks to an erroneous attribution, her most frequently quoted line. She never dared correct the misunderstanding. It hounded her when she won those prizes. It plagued her on the death of the stepdaughter she'd cared for as her own, and even when her own death started nipping at her heels. As soon as anything receded into the past, she realized that she actually enjoyed her friends' mistakes, enjoyed contributing to the demolition of the young man who approached her as she prattled on in a corner of the hall, enjoyed pronouncing stark truths that caused the ruin of her loved ones.

I put down the letter, half-read—I couldn't take any more of her whining—and glanced at her motionless body. Then I opened all the little wooden doors in the room that had been her workplace for so many years. I stared at the spines of the notebooks. They covered more than an entire wall, overflowing from the shelves she'd built herself, hidden behind the books. She always used the same kind of notebook at first, but they soon started changing size and color. There was a thick-notebook period and a small-and-thin-notebook period. Later, she'd settled on a specific kind of notebook that was bound in bluish leather and ruled with lines that were far too wide for her tiny script.

I sat down in her reading chair, switched on the lamp, and started paging through them. The same stories were repeated over and over in different syntax, in different words intentionally overlaid with contradictory meanings. She omitted information that appeared later on, or rearranged events out of order, or included explanations where there had previously been none. The stories grew longer and more complex. Then they shrank down until they all seemed like the very same story endlessly written and rewritten. In the last notebooks, the stories morphed into mere lines, as if marking her mental activity in waves, peaks, and valleys, grounded in nothing but the green strokes of a pen on paper.

I was supposed to organize the funeral. She'd made the request in writing, the lawyers told me that night. This information and her other wishes lured journalists like wayward men bewitched by siren songs. Disputes with the leaders of the writer's sect were made public. Under the dark tunics and demonic masks they used to conceal their identities, they declared that her body must be buried without pollutants:

naked and alone. No one but they must know the location of her grave, and no mark or fire must inscribe it. After a long discussion among the lawyers, trying to avert a scandal, and after various intrusions by the literary milieu and the fans amassing outside what had been the writer's home, but now served as storage for my furniture, I managed to orchestrate her cremation behind everyone else's backs and attended it as a spectator.

"One cold winter evening, I stood before the snow-white body of the writer and watched it blaze inside a concrete grid." So begins my prologue to the edition of her *Dirty Notebooks*, which is how I chose to title the anthology of her posthumous work.

Cristián

I hadn't read the obituaries in decades. When you live in an adopted country, when you're an exile in your own body, names are simply lists that dull the reality of death. At the age of eleven, when I was still living in Chile and hadn't yet fully lost my eyesight, I'd read every word. I'd squint at the page, hoping to absorb those lives before they slipped away from me. Maybe catching a glimpse of their crimes, loves, triumphs, and downfalls would help me shake the fragility I felt, the darkness clouding my vision. Later, living in the shadows, I'd learn that obituaries are where lives muffle to a murmur.

Just a few moments ago, I got a call from an old classmate of mine, someone I've more or less kept up with over the years. She urged me to open the local newspaper to the obituary section. Quickly realizing her mistake, she read the list of deaths aloud to me, her voice loud, as if my ears were defective as well. I listened intently as she told me that another grade-school acquaintance of ours, this one blurrier and more distant in my memory, was the one who'd informed her that our other classmate, Cristián, had died in the city where I now live. She hoped, and everyone agreed, that I would attend the funeral as a representative of this stage of his life.

As I listened to her voice on the other end of the line, I heard his, rising up from roll call. That must have been how I met him: through his name, spoken aloud by our teacher. I would have forgotten his face—I've forgotten everyone else's—if it hadn't burned itself onto my retina during a childhood fever.

When I was nine years old, I contracted an illness that kept me paralyzed and bedridden for over two months. The virus set up camp in my head and proceeded to take over the rest of my body, sparking the first indications of decline. I could see perfectly then. I spent most of every day in my mother's bed, staring at a TV set my father had forgotten to take with him when he left. During those months, which I still remember vividly, I'd watch my mother as she got ready for work, parted the curtains, pulled open the windows, and gave me a goodbye kiss on the forehead. A long silence echoed once she was gone, and I'd wander my thoughts, travel the shapes and colors of my simmering body.

I remember the penstrokes my mother made on a sheet of paper—instructions for the woman who looked after me—and how the letters suddenly seemed to materialize on the bathroom door, across the hall, which swelled closer and loomed over my bed until it burst inside my skull. The woman who looked after me would try to calm me down by holding out some water for me to sip. Around noon, she'd sit down beside me and switch the channel to a soap opera about a young woman from a rural village who'd gotten a job as a maid for a wealthy family in the capital. Her life was an endless spate of misfortunes. Her first disaster struck when she fell in love with her young master. He was engaged to a woman who wore expensive low-necked dresses, high heels, lip liner, and eye shadow, a woman who dyed her hair the blackest of blacks and had a harsh accent and a pompous last name. Peering into windows, mirrors, and corners, the enemy eye surveyed the young woman as she cleaned, cooked, scrubbed floors, and took care of the child. The mansion had a big black gate and a perfect garden that suffused the place with the ominous air of a slave plantation or a jail. The heroine's only source of solace was her boss's kid brother—because, even though no one else understood her, even though her employers exploited her, hit her, and subjected her broken heart to endless humiliations, the boy was always ready with a wise word to remind her that life was beautiful. This boy reminded me of Cristián. They shared a slight oral disfigurement, moderate childhood obesity, and a nasal voice. I hated the duplicitous virtue of the onscreen character, his utter lack of insight, his flair for manipulation, his indifference to his own violent relatives. More than anything, I hated that he was a terrible actor and yet persisted in occupying my visual field, monopolizing my attention. The boy was, I thought in my spasms of fever, the core, the very bedrock sustaining the long conspiracy of injustices called life and melodrama. I started to hate Cristián.

One day, when my head was about to explode and my body was refusing both food and liquid, the woman who looked after me left me alone with the TV on. As always, the heroine of the soap opera took the little boy to the playground. Those were her happiest moments. The boy was happy, too, and his blurry smile fogged up the frame. Lying completely still, I could see him on the tiny screen from the corner of a feverish eye. With the other eye, I checked to make sure the bathroom door wasn't going to swallow me whole. Roaming free, the boy climbed the jungle gym and fumbled his way around the ropes. He waved to his nanny from the top of the slide as the sun streamed around him, haloing him like a saint. Seeing her future in him, the young maid no longer cared what the other women murmured behind her back. She no longer cared that her employers struck her at work. She only had eyes for the child who wasn't hers, the child she'd never have with the man she couldn't help but love. There he was, the little boy, with his faint resemblance to the rakish figures that had stolen her heart. And through the boy's eyes, the man could also see that she was a good woman, that her poverty was a fluke of circumstance, that her veins coursed with aristocratic blood. She waved back to the boy, drunk on her good fortune. I closed my eyes, overcome with repulsion, mustering all my strength to shove at the door that tried again and again to crush me under its weight. When I returned to the screen, the little boy was lying on the ground, his head motionless in a pool of blood and muddy water. The heroine begged the other women for help as she cradled the boy's head and Cristián's life trickled away. The door finally collapsed and shattered over me. I vomited onto the covers.

After that day, my fever broke and my vision started to blur. I went back to school a few weeks later. The teacher took attendance and Cristián responded to his name, monstrous and alive. I eventually got used to his presence there. We grew up together. I learned to separate the things my mind had fused. But whenever the corner of my nearly sightless eye caught a glimpse of Cristián's still-long or just-cut hair, whenever I accepted a pencil from his clammy, clumsy hand, my fever returned. Whenever he spoke in front of the class, whenever he hit a weaker classmate on the playground, whenever he mocked his best friends as we filed out of the building for the day, I remembered what had died along with that character in the park, at the foot of the slide, in the arms of a maid who'd just arrived from the village. I discovered this as he obsessively tackled difficult math problems, when he declared his interest in economy, when the size of his bank account determined that he would attend a prestigious American college and get married, it didn't really matter to whom.

I couldn't even forget it when I went completely blind. I never got to see him kiss the wife he'd selected for the biography he'd calculated as meticulously as a screenplay, or to confirm whether his children were the spitting image of the Cristián branded onto my retina. But when I offered each of them my condolences at the funeral, I felt the same damp fingers leave their sour scent on mine.

The Student

When I returned to the university, convinced I'd left the night-mare behind, I sank into the armchair in my office. There was a knock on the door. I sighed. It was his mother. She sat down on the only other chair, facing me from the other side of the desk, exactly where the student himself had sat, moments before he'd fallen to the ground, dead. I offered her a box of Kleenex to feign discomfort. She tugged a tissue out and dabbed at her eyes, glancing sidelong at the boarded window, the bullet hole still visible. I was the last person to see him as she would have wanted him to be seen, she explained. Now it was impossible: the legal process, the photos, the morgue, the rash of newspaper articles. She described what had happened in recent months, avoiding any information that didn't cor-respond to the image of the beaming student on the protest signs. She wanted to know the details. I paused for a moment, collecting the papers that had lain scattered all over the desk for months now. I touched my wedding band. Suddenly exhausted, my brain hunted for any intentions she may have concealed in her furtive visit. Her son's last words—how could I explain this to her without everything else tumbling out of me like a waterfall?—hadn't emerged from his mouth. They were more like projectiles fired by his eyes, his hand.

Last semester I had to teach a class in which we were supposed to talk about a vast array of issues and nothing in particular. More than a course, it seemed like an excuse to kill time and give grades. It was certainly the easiest class for his fellow students. And so, having moved to this country a few months earlier for a teaching job with some decent health insurance and, therefore, a chance to heal from my mysterious ailment that no doctor had managed to diagnose, I'd pause to talk about politics in hopes of exorcising the image of the Great Wall that tormented me at night and followed me on my daytime walks along the cicada-dense New Jersey streets. These topics immediately divided the classroom. Only a few students listened in silence, staring down at the distracted lines they traced in their notebooks. Some spoke in support of state laws that forbade immigrants from living and working in the area. They even supported militarization as a way to do away with the protests in the city. Others seethed as they recounted how hard it was to commute to school without getting stopped and registered by the police. A group of students had decided to confront the situation head-on and swiftly ended up in jail or hospitalized with tear gas exposure. Two from the group were in our class.

I couldn't say it was because of me. It was the noise that filtered in through the classroom window, the blue police uniforms, the security barriers, the constant ID checks, how the word "terrorism" proliferated and suffused the halls. The student assembly issued a statement against the possession and use of firearms. Fear, the letter argued, had prompted many young people to keep guns and razors in their dorm rooms, triggering massive raids. Several of my students were subjected to them, mainly first-generation immigrants. And him, as I recall. Even so, the student was muted in his opinions, almost crushingly levelheaded in the face of it all.

During this time, a group of protestors held a rally at the entrance of our building, right outside the classroom window. Less than two hours later, a police car with tinted windows parked on the front walkway. Tensions rose when another group of young people gathered nearby with banners calling for freedom and the right to bear arms. From then on, our conversations centered on freedom, its roots and definitions, its limitations and uses. On whether it meant something different in our own everyday context. By that point, no one remained apathetic, and our intense debates in Spanish encompassed radically divergent opinions. The student spoke up that day. For them, he explained, freedom was defined by whoever pulled a weapon first. The classroom seemed to embody that freedom for a couple of weeks, the student said on another occasion, as we heard the periodic rumble of bombs and explosions beyond the buildings and courtyards.

Until the gun appeared. It was the day I couldn't make it to class because the security guards who searched us at the entrance decided that my faculty ID was inadequate. They demanded to see my passport and my visa. Unconvinced, they compared the colors in the photo to the hues of my face. The student and some of his classmates had leaned out the windows for a better view, their bodies all but hanging in midair. When I finally reached the classroom, covering my face, coughing from the tear gas that had sent several protestors into spasms outside, we watched together as the police continued to disperse the protesters, now with physical force. The young people's bodies were hauled off by four police officers and stuffed into a truck like rag dolls, watermelons, sacks of hay. In an impromptu staff meeting in the hallway of the Spanish department, we decided to resume our classes and talk about Latin American food, traditions, and regional dances, steadying our own tremors and paranoia with our heads lowered and our traps shut. When I returned to the classroom and started in again, I felt the student's look of disappointment like a mirror.

He followed me. Standing in the hall outside the Spanish department, we watched in silence as a strange woman inspected my file cabinets. Without crossing the threshold, he handed me his essay, which he'd revised according to my feedback. I reached for the papers as my eyes tracked the woman. But the student wouldn't let go of them. He waited for my gaze to rest on the essay, on his hands, and rise up his arm, his neck, the taut muscles of his face, all the way to his eyes. For an instant, he seemed older. Only then did he release his grip, turn away, and walk out of the building.

A deathly silence governed the last week of the semester. My colleagues' text messages and email notifications rattled my phone. That afternoon, the student appeared a few minutes before I left my office to go home. He sat down across from me, on the other side of the desk. It took him a while to locate the zipper on his backpack. Another email alert cut into our silence, then the secretary's voice on the phone outside the office. When I looked up, the student had a gun in his hands. He placed it gently on the desk. It's my treasure, he said to me in Spanish, and he moved my phone away from me. The door was barely ajar enough for me to see people moving around at the end of the hall. It was about the topic of his final paper. That was what he'd come to discuss. I heard the fragile filament of my own voice. I didn't have to finish my sentence. There were no bullets in it, he said. Suddenly, the ambient noise returned, my ears unplugged, bombs blasted again in the distance. With my vision re-focused, I noticed the police lights shifting across the office walls, slinging light onto his face and white T-shirt. My fingers instinctively touched the ring on my left hand. He interrupted my gesture with his right, whispering, Okay, maybe just one, and held out the papers to me. I took them, slowly peeling myself away from his touch, but the student didn't let go until my foggy eyes met his once more.

The crack of the gun surprised us both. I touched my neck and felt the shrill pain of embedded glass. Blood trickled. The student had taken his hand off mine. His weight and the force of the impact firing in through the window had thrust the chair away from my desk. He was slumped to one side and his arm was flung up over his face, a hand still clutching his Spanish-language essay.

I left the office. The people who'd thrown themselves under tables called an ambulance as soon as they saw the blood streaming down my neck. Given the clashes and the barricades, the vehicle took over two hours to arrive. Sitting in the secretary's chair, where I'd been asked to wait, I looked down at the red-spattered floor. I was wrong: he hadn't covered his head. The impact had torn it off. In the days that followed, the police had demanded I clarify this part of my testimony, but I found myself unable to rectify what I saw, to make it make sense. It was a jumble, the violence. What I didn't tell them is that I'd walked over to his body, carefully wrapped his gun in a handkerchief, put it in his backpack, removed the papers from his languid fingers, and slipped them into their folder.

Those were the things that came to mind as my mouth refrained from telling his mother the details of our semester. No one ever brought up the gun in his backpack. I was too scared to mention it and the police never asked. The silence was a conspiracy. The student had been the victim of a stray bullet, fired by an older man of unknown origin who had, in a trance, taken advantage of the chaos. That was the official version, as reported by the press.

My hands closed into fists on the desk as the mother flipped through all the papers that had earned the student high grades. They all involved regional dishes, traditional dances, or Latin American myths. All of his words matched the white teeth and innocent eyes displayed by the paltry crowd railing outside the courtroom doors. Just one man would be judged. The mother offered me her hands, which were cold as iron, and stroked mine in a gesture of gratitude. Then my vision blurred and the sounds faded away. In the secretary's chair, where I tried to steady my breath, I considered giving her the last essay the student had written.

The Head

In memory of Susana Rothker and Tomás Eloy Martínez

A memory sprang to mind as she sat down in her office chair. It was something that had happened the day before, but it transported her to decades past. She opened the sliding door and stepped out onto the deck, as she usually did on Sundays. She picked up the newspaper and her tea mug, looking out at the roofs of the houses that sprouted up like orderly mushrooms in the woods of the highest hill on the highest plot of land in the New Jersey suburbs. She recalled her satisfaction as if it were the backdrop for a hard-earned act of revenge, but the feeling dissolved at the sight of her neighbors' red car. They were Russian, and they'd just moved into the most opulent house in the neighborhood, settled grandly among the cypresses and American elms. She immediately wrote to her sister, the only person—they say—who ever understood the essays of interiority encoded in her texts. Receiving no response, her sense of complacency shifted into something external, morphing slowly into a shadow in the window, over her shoulder, behind her back. It appeared as often as it escaped her when she tried to look at it head-on. She couldn't be sure—which drove her crazy, they say—whether the shadow wore the familiar face and smug look she'd so often observed in the mirror hanging in a corner of her office.

Her steps echoed through the old house where the Spanish department was headquartered. Every so often, colleagues, students, secretaries, administrators, and technicians would peek in to see if she was still pacing around. People on the first floor attested to the reliably peculiar attitude of the department head: she'd ask in passing if they hadn't by any chance received a message from her sister by mistake. The boldest among them even returned the question: When did you write to her? Or, where is your sister? Or, what did you write her about? Or, did you use the right keyboard? The department head was inconsistent in her answers. Although, some explained, the head sometimes replied that she—sometimes her sister, sometimes her—had just gotten on a flight to Mexico. Or she—sometimes her sister, sometimes the head herself—had just returned from a trip to Peru.

Just after 1 P.M., everyone saw a PhD student venture through the door of the Spanish department and hurry upstairs, carrying seven books and a truly enormous umbrella under various handbags and vests. She barely acknowledged the staff, congregated on the first floor like an audience on the verge of uncovering a secret, or the racket on the second floor. The young woman's air of nonchalance raised more than a couple eyebrows. Only once she'd reached the top of the stairs did the PhD student excuse herself with a downward glance: she was late for a meeting with the department head. On the first floor, everyone held their breath. Some swore they didn't exhale until the PhD student came back down the stairs less than an hour later.

Later that day, ashen faced, the PhD student sat down in the miniscule conference room, surrounded by her purses, books, coats, notepads, papers, wool scarves, feathers, and other useless accessories. In her testimony, which was recorded, transcribed, and analyzed, she recounted how the head had waved her into the office without lifting her eyes from an old newspaper announcing the destruction of the Berlin Wall. The head asked if the PhD student understood how it had changed the world. But then she backtracked. Of course, she said, the PhD student couldn't know much at all, because she was very young and still didn't have any sort of well-informed political perspective. The student responded that she had actually been paying quite a lot of attention when the Wall came down. In fact, it had radically transformed her own life. The head nodded, not listening. She asked the PhD student if she knew any protest songs, and then she herself began to hum and wander around the office. The young woman glanced at the clock and gathered her nerve to ask whether there was any other way the head could offer her another year of financial support. The head shook her head no.

An uncomfortable silence filled the conference room, where these events were described. Meanwhile, the PhD student mentally calculated how she was going to pay for the health insurance that had forced her to leave her home country for a place as sinister as New Jersey, and whether she'd even be able to feed herself as she frenetically cranked out articles and talks and the dissertation she always presented with the blank look of someone who'd had her fill.

"Well," the head interrupted, "there are very few alternatives. And all are for American candidates with acceptable but imperfect Spanish."

Then, the testimony continued, the head tried to interest her in taking a few classes on literature and social movements that were offered by a competent professor on staff, the very same professor who was finally going to publish a fascinating and consequential study on poverty in Spain. These classes would be accessible for an in-state fee. The PhD student reminded her, not without shedding a tear that everyone in the miniscule conference room and the curious onlookers peering in through the windows interpreted as a tear of guilt, that she was finishing her dissertation and didn't need to take any more classes. So the head offered to put in a good word so she'd get the class that nobody wanted but everybody needed, except for the head. Besides, the head insisted, no one should leave New Jersey without trying the organic mushrooms that grew on the highest point on campus. Everyone in the conference room suddenly felt a pang of hunger.

That afternoon, the secretary was the last to leave the building. The next day, she testified, once she'd finished cleaning up the lunch leftovers that the professors had left behind after the PhD student's interrogation—an event that more than one had mistaken for some kind of party—she'd gone upstairs to shut the windows. She cautiously brought her ear to the office door. The sounds were otherworldly. She heard, instead of the ceaseless click-clack of the head's shoes, a pack of small animals, as if the squirrels that inhabited the American elms had suddenly invaded the small wooden house where the Spanish department was headquartered. The pack went silent when a floorboard creaked under the secretary's weight. She grazed the office door with her pinky finger and it swung open. The head was sitting bolt upright in her leather chair and smiling radiantly. The secretary testified that they laughed for a long while. She took it, of course, as a good omen.

The head was in a cheerful mood. She invited the secretary to sit down across from her desk. She told the secretary about joining the student marches and about the time when a classmate gave her her first orgasm on top of the protest signs they were painting. She talked about the time she attended an assembly and got into an argument with a member of the radical homosexual collective because he'd inadvertently sprayed her dark hair with saliva during a declamation. She talked about the time she'd lost the election to her Red Party opponent, because she'd incorrectly interpreted Marx in the debate by incorrectly citing Gramsci. She talked about the time after that when she'd led a resistance movement and had even written a poem and set it to music, although she'd never been able to sing it properly. She almost convinced the secretary to listen to it, so that the secretary could decide whether she'd been mistaken in abandoning her career as an artist of the revolution and dedicating her life to fricatives instead. But the secretary, glancing at the clock, kindly suggested postponing this performance until they had access to a guitar.

As the secretary delivered her testimony, the second-floor halls filled with shouts, wails, and murmurs. As always, the PhD students were the last to hear the news. One of them even threw up his instant dinner, which he'd all but inhaled the night before as he graded a hundred papers he'd only been able to stomach by drinking straight from a transparent bottle of something, when he heard that, beyond the yellow police tape, the head had committed a poetic act by cutting off her own head.

The Ghost

The last time I saw him, he was sitting in an armchair in one of those chain cafés in a swanky Barrio Alto mall, in Santiago. It was early, so only the employees were moving around under the cold light as it reflected off the glassy tiles. I went in fifteen minutes after opening and he was already there, like a ghost, the only customer in the whole place. At the register, I accidentally dropped some money into my shopping bags and the bills scattered among the contents: new light bulbs, candles. He watched me out of the corner of his eye, my things taking on that vague morning smell of bleach and dirty mop. When I turned around, coffee in hand, his eyes were low in a book taken from the tower he'd stacked up on the corner of the table. I could see it was an interpretative essay on Freud and Lacan, which is what he studied in hopes of incorporating it into the psychoanalytic therapy that had left him completely mute.

He greeted me with a nod.

Back then, he never stopped talking. We never stopped talking about books.

The question that arises, and which indeed all Freud's previous indications allow us here to produce, is—What is it that wakes the sleeper? Is it not, in the dream, another reality?—the reality that Freud describes thus: that the child is near the father's bed, takes him by the arm, and whispers to him reproachfully, Father, can't you see that I am burning?

The first time I saw him was under a single light bulb, facing a microphone, telling the whole school we weren't worth shit. It was around 1990, and he was the only student who exercised his right to take the floor, which was theoretically available to us in our general assemblies—a mysterious idea cooked up by the school authorities to provide some semblance of liberty to those of us who'd never experienced it before. But that stonewalled society, which confined our fields of study, play, and seduction, cemented fears that our blackboards would come to snap the chain-like nerves that had been forged in the militaristic realism of the Chilean right.

The phantom is the work in the unconscious of the inadmissible secret of an Other. Its manifestation, as anxiety, is the return of the phantom in bizarre words and acts and symptoms.

Not long before, I'd seen him in a similar café, in another mall, drinking milky coffee with an astonishing amount of sugar, two books tucked under his arm. And before that, I'd seen him in my bedroom, his face marked by pain or pleasure, I could never tell which.

As we always did when we saw each other, we talked about books that morning. Tight-lipped as he'd become, I talked far more than he did, until he excused himself and emerged a few minutes later from the bathroom, trailing the stench of weed. The café employees were so used to his presence that they didn't even react.

Despite all these phantasmagorical visits experienced during sleep, he wakes with a clearer, more resolute mind.

I can still see him stepping barefoot along the rocky shore and into the lake, blue trunks, long hair, a bandanna of the same color dropping to the ground. He wore it like Axl Rose even after we'd forgotten the singer and his leather jackets with no T-shirt underneath. The same skinniness, the same femininity. I was so young that I mistook his affectation for rigor. When I saw him, fifteen years later, sitting in an easy chair with a haircut, underlining psychology books, as if the very act of reading could construct a world he'd lost in every glimmer of sunlight, I could see how fragile he was. I didn't recognize myself. Even so, I said goodbye as I always had. I kept searching for the shameless kid who'd sat down across from me and my mother, high out of his mind, to confess that he loved me. My skin then was bronzed by the sun of a beach where my friend's brother had undressed me and kissed my breasts while her other brother alerted the entire household. In the ghost's confession, I only heard desire. By the next day, his words had abandoned him.

Awakening, in Lacan's reading of the dream, is itself the site of a trauma, the trauma of the necessity and impossibility of responding to another's death. To awaken is thus precisely to awaken only to one's repetition of a previous failure to see in time.

Years later, in a similar psychotropic episode, he and his friends left my brother without his wallet, phone, keys, or jacket in a bar miles from home. No one knew where he was until the next day, when he turned up pale and hollow-eyed after walking all night long. My mother blamed the ghost, who had so often sat around drinking whiskey at our place. Even so, she went with my brother when we learned that his best friend had died under peculiar circumstances.

We must analyze the abrupt awakening of other horizons that manifest themselves in the same word and which must lead to other unspeakable catastrophes that have occurred in the lives of others, in a beyond-myself. In this other life and in this other topic, the other horizons of the same word, its secret horizons, are destined for non-existence, for silence, for death without a burial.

Not long before he met his end, his psychoanalyst, also a martial arts expert, was arrested for stabbing a young man in the belly in the doorway of a party where the psychoanalyst worked as a security guard. We could only watch how it happened on TV and in pieces: we beheld a body deformed by excessive exercise and food, his head shaved to the scalp. Years prior, the psychoanalyst had organized a Lacan study group at his house. He'd been fired from the university and banned from the psychoanalytical association for strange reasons he recounted with laughter and the ghost insistently defended. The home where the Lacanian psychoanalyst held his study group, I determined over the couple months of my attendance, was a dimming promise. His wife had left him. His young daughters divided their time between the school bus and a silent second floor. Sometimes the power was out. On other occasions, a maid would open the door for us and bring in glasses of water and then be gone the next week. The psychoanalyst's house, high on a hillside miles from the bus we took to get there, was in an up-and-coming neighborhood that had never finished coming up. The red tiles stained our shoes, so our footprints marked the concrete when we filed out after our sessions. One week, a puppy appeared. Stroking his head, I realized his ears were newly mutilated, the scabs crumbling into my hands. I never saw him again. Apparently, the dog grew dangerous. There was nothing special about the living room where we met: dark walls, semi-new furniture, a plant or two, paintings with dense brushstrokes. One day the walls were bare: empty rectangles stood out against the reddish paint where things had once been. When I decided to leave the study group, I sent the psychoanalyst a handwritten letter. He had my brother tell me to visit him, for a reason I decided, shivering, that I wanted to know nothing else about. My brother soon stopped going, too. Sometime later, still in therapy, the ghost went essentially mute.

My brother would often tell me when we spoke on the phone that the ghost was now living with a friend, a girl who'd been his classmate at the university. They'd both studied psychology but neither had graduated. She inherited two adjacent houses and a fortune after her father died. At the same time, he'd discovered in therapy that being adopted had haunted him with a constant sense of abandonment. He was incredibly thin. She was obese. The heiress's house—they invited me over once—had thick, dusty curtains and velvet-upholstered furniture, also coated in dust, with feet that sank into a lumpy carpet. It was like an abandoned basement.

To some people the idea of being buried alive by mistake is the most uncanny thing of all. And yet psycho-analysis has taught us that this terrifying phantasy is only a transformation of another phantasy which had originally nothing terrifying about it at all, but was qualified by a certain lasciviousness—the phantasy, I mean, of intra-uterine existence.

The owner of the house had a boyfriend who looked exactly like the two or three friends who were always with him. They all wore black jeans, dark T-shirts with satanic white faces, and black sneakers. They drank *pisco* and Coke. None of them had a job or went to school, but they had luxurious objects strapped to their wrists and tucked into their pockets. The house had several stories and a cellar divided into small concrete rooms with no windows or flooring. They were just concrete blocks inhabited by some spartan furniture. A few months later, the rooms were occupied by two classmates of the heiress's from the university, one schizophrenic, the other afflicted by a constant sense of abandonment. I imagine there were probably also books in the ghost's room.

Analysis can throw light on such an affect but, far from insisting on breaking it down, it should make way for esthetics (some might add philosophy), with which to saturate its phantasmal progression and insure its cathartic eternal return.

My brother told me, curt, his voice hoarser than usual, that the ghost had died from asphyxiation, staring up at the light.

When we were all still young and lived in the protection of our parents' homes, there were things the ghost would always keep on his bedside table: an ashtray, a pipe, a pack of cigarettes or two, tobacco, marijuana, rolling paper, a lighter, a candle, incense sticks, and an incense holder. Despite the lung scans, my brother said, he'd never kicked the habit.

He was found on the floor, the candle burned down, the mattress half-charred, a blow to the head from where he'd fallen.

The Patient

She woke that morning to the caws of the crows on her windowsill. She wandered around my office as if inspecting every detail, trailing one of her wool scarves, dangling pompoms. I told her that was why most patients ended up here. She shot me a reproving glare through her thick blue frames. I offered to hang up her coat, but a leather-gloved gesture made it clear that she'd rather keep her belongings close by. She took a few moments to settle into her chair, skittishly rearranging her layers, her scarves, hides, feathers, bags. She pulled off her hat with lace-sheathed fingers and twisted her hair into a nest on top of her head. She started speaking with a perverse kind of nonchalance, as she did in her well-known lectures and talks.

She said: I don't like being compared to other people. All this talk of how every experience is just as ordinary as any other—it's a pointless way of resigning yourself to being yourself. I'd rather die if that were true.

Her speech wasn't fluid or relaxed. She forced her consonants against her small teeth. As I took notes, she fixed her eyes on the shelves where I kept, among other things, my psychology books.

That's why I started writing. Novels, the best novels, explore the singularity of our perceptions. That sensation, whether it makes us feel part of something or inspires total indifference, is what people are looking for when they open a book.

Two hands, bony as claws, clutched at the bags in her lap. The bags looked heavy, as if they were full of gold ingots.

Some people might read them for entertainment.

That must be why you read novels, she retorted, drawing out the *you* like an owl and tilting her head toward one of the shelves. Have you read them all?

Yes.

And you found them entertaining.

She stretched her words. I couldn't tell if it was a question or a statement.

Some of them, yes.

Almost no one has read all the books they own.

Have you?

She paused before answering, as if she'd tripped on some syllables poised on the tip of her tongue.

I've practiced many kinds of reading. I've spent quite some time looking for the same thing in every book, something indescribable. If it doesn't appear in the first few pages, I'll flip through the rest without even reading them. Some books are only good for steadying the crooked leg of a table. And when I find what I'm looking for, I have to stop and take in every word, savor them slowly, absorb them with total intensity among other, lesser books.

Does it bother you when you can't describe something in words?

No. Her accent was hard to place. It's part of how I survive. At least at this point in my life.

And what point is that?, we said almost in unison, with the same inflection, though hers was sarcastic and mine sincere. She crowned our chorus with a harsh bark of laughter, as if to say: sometimes the words flow out of us according to plan, like a mere replica. Didn't I know that, after so many years of practice? I'd heard the same words used again and again to explain the most disparate circumstances. For decades, the medical profession had been perfecting a system to simplify the scale with which patients measure and express physical discomfort. Is it a sharp pain? A sense of heat spreading across a large area? Or do you feel as if your flesh were burning with intense cold? Or maybe it's like a knife were slicing into your skin and advancing slowly into your ribcage? Take a close look at the Wong-Baker scale, the EVA chart, the Pfeiffer SPMSQ questionnaire, the Karnofsky scale, the Mankoski scale, the McGill questionnaire, the IPAT, the FLACC. How would you describe the pain you feel when something's tearing your chest open and you think you're about to die?

I'm here to explore the ways I can express pain. The woman interrupted my thoughts, looking serious. To compose a complex score of its gradations. Look, doctor, I've spent my whole life writing about pain. I've chiseled out a written voice, a voice that's controlled in every way. I can use words, channel them with my own hands, and glaze them with polished wisdom. I can, if you prefer, entertain my readers with other people's pain, which is what the books on those shelves of yours do. But now I'm here to learn from our oral exchange.

I was going to ask her something, but she didn't even notice.

I'm here in search of a place to experiment with this trembling, childlike voice of mine, to talk my way into a tone I've never found, to strike the perfect chord in saying what's never before been said between two people. Is this a reasonable objective for someone in your line of work?

Within seconds, I'd assessed the dame with medical eyes, with a man's eyes, with the eyes of someone who's read all the books the patient ever wrote. A thought came to me, utterly clear: will I ever be able to look at anything again as if for the first time. She'd chosen this particular staging for her experiment, motivated, perhaps, by our obvious age difference, by my credentials, and by the positive comments other patients had posted on my public profile. Did she know her way around that kind of technology? The wrinkles on her face sometimes seemed to vanish altogether. Her hands looked as if they'd borne those knuckles for a century, and her eyes assessed me with real hunger. A coil of her hair rested on a corner of the table. Curled there, it looked like a tangled little nest. She tossed me a devilish, adolescent look from her chair.

46

If you agree, then I'd like to start right away.

She peered into one of her bags and pulled out a small leather sack. She fingered it obscenely for a moment, then dropped it open onto the table between us. A thick bundle of hundred-dollar bills slipped gently out of it.

This is what I'm offering you. You'll have to accept it as willingly as a prostitute accepts her charge.

My brow furrowed, stopping her.

Prostitution is nothing to be ashamed of, Dr. Segal. It's much like work in every way. And workers should never be ashamed of what they do to support themselves. The people who pay are the ones who should be ashamed of their need to exploit.

And you're not ashamed.

You and I both know that I've exerted a certain power over you ever since I stepped into this office. Ever since I made an appointment and gave you my name. You've been waiting for me, you've prepared for our session, you've hidden my novels on one of these shelves. And you've been observing me, you've been wondering about my clothes. I'm sure you've noticed that I pick them out every morning with great care. And so do you. I noticed it as soon as I set eyes on you a few months ago, at that awards ceremony at the university. That's one of the reasons why I chose you. You're pleasant to look at. That, and the shine of your hair.

The patient's lusty smile broadened as she followed the arc of my hand, which I could no longer control, as it reached up to touch my own hair, swept up into a quiff and fixed in place with gel.

What are the other reasons?

Her smile disappeared, as if the question had disappointed her somehow.

Your age. Also, you don't speak my mother tongue, which leaves me no choice but to address you in this foreign language. You have no idea how hard it is to find someone who doesn't speak Spanish in this city.

I'm interested in why you enjoy comparing any job to prostitution.

She tilted her head to one side. Maybe they're simply words stripped of meaning.

In other words, you strip people's words of their meaning in your novels?

But you have so many printed words hanging up in elegant frames. They speak for you. All those titles on the shelves that declare your identity, your profession, your knowledge, your ascent up the social ladder. And your designer clothes broadcast the money you've got at your disposal. Besides, that voice of yours, so steady and controlled, is remarkable in someone so young. If you devoted yourself to prostitution, you'd be a consummate professional.

I'm not sure I can help you.

Years ago, I lost interest in my work for a while. When I opened a recently published novel, I'd see that it was something I'd read many times. But then I started to appreciate the pleasure of rediscovering the same thing over and over. It's a feeling that some of my more devotedly careerist colleagues have never even experienced. Many of them truly believed that the discipline was all about being disciplined.

She froze as if she'd thought of someone.

Do you write every day?

I can be disciplined, yes. But I've always liked to do lots of different things at the same time, and all of those activities have always struck me as equally important, no matter how unproductive they may be. I can't imagine writing without that impulse. How can you take time to write if you're struggling to feed yourself and keep a roof over your head?

But you don't have to worry about that anymore.

Once again, she ignored my interruption. How, she continued, if you're answerable to so much pressure in this world? If you have to satisfy the demands of coworkers, bosses, students? Isn't our session almost over?

But you left this sack on the coffee table.

Maybe I want to feel like I'm running out of time. Maybe my sense of well-being depends on it. Patience isn't my forte.

Maybe you don't want to be my patient, I wanted to snap, although I was distracted by a trace of Grand Cru by Romanée-Conti drifting out of the little leather bag.

I hated sitting in your waiting room. Please don't make me do that ever again.

You didn't find it comfortable enough?

A waiting room is never comfortable enough. It's designed to be miserable. Waiting isn't purgatory, it's hell. All those vapid magazines, that pensive music, those chairs that make your legs sweat.

You read the Bible.

I'm from Latin America, doctor. Even if we don't read the Bible or Dante, we know everything about those books. Who among us can say they understand every word ever written? No one, ever.

So you don't think literature is important.

It depends on what you want to do with it.

Offer someone money, for example?

I've offended you. Is it too small a sum?

On the contrary. Wasn't your intention to destroy something between us before it had even begun?

To what end?

To transform the possibilities for interrelation that this office allows.

There's a limit to what money can control.

But it's a binding contract, this money.

Like every signed piece of paper in the world. Do you have any of my novels?

Would you like to sign it?

I want to know which one you decided to read.

I hesitated for a moment. But I was already on my feet, fastening the two buttons on my jacket, as my tailor had instructed me. I pulled out a volume concealed behind the psychology manuals, and she took it, adjusting her glasses. She read the title as she cracked her nightmarish knuckles, revealing crimson-painted nails through the lace webbing of her gloves. She flipped through the pages as if reviewing the content of a book she'd never seen before, analyzing its properties to determine whether it was worth buying or not.

Are you satisfied with it?

Are you?

It's a good novel, like any other.

You won that prize for it. It made you who you are today.

Maybe it made me into this novel.

Your work is very powerful. Why do you feel the need to treat it with contempt?

For the same reason why anyone treats anything with contempt. I told you at the beginning of the session. Maybe it's the caws of the crows in the morning, maybe it's the snow I see through my window, maybe it's because I talk as if I were giving one of my lectures.

Are you talking about your life or about literature?

Is there a difference?

I spied another tangled lock of black hair in a corner of the office.

One of them is your job.

When I first moved to this country, countless decades ago, I remember reading about how art as life had ended when the last poets died out. But that's not true. Journalists don't understand it, scientists don't understand it.

And you expect me to understand it.

Maybe if you take the money.

We can talk about it in our next session, I told her, and I tucked the bills, except for two, back into the little sack. The leather was incredibly delicate to the touch. Please don't forget this, I urged, holding it out to her.

She didn't take it. She was busy stuffing herself back into every article of clothing she'd scattered over the chair. It took her some time to put on her jacket with its little hooks, her wool shawl, her leather coat with its four rows of buttons, and then her various belts and sashes, an industrially woven scarf, a pair of leather gloves that fit over her lace ones, and then the feathers for her hair and her hands. As she adjusted her hat, I was finally able to shake the anxiety that had overtaken me at the first glimpse of her nest-like bun. And so, entirely covered up, she looked at me and said, See you next week, then went out, sweeping away the stray curls strewn across my office floor with the long wool tassel of her scarf.

She'd left the money. I sat down to examine the contents of the sack. As the sun vanished and the city lights shone onto the streets and the river like stars of the underworld, I took out a box and wrote her name on it, stacking it on the shelf along with all my other patients' boxes.

Dead Men Don't Rape

En el año 2020, escribí for the man with hands like a squirrel:

Mr. Speechifier, Vice-President, members and members of the members; people peering through jail-bars, through border-fences, through TV screens; my fellow citizens and those who are citizens no longer: I am here to inform you that the financial crisis has evaporated into thin air and that, having excised 45% of the illegal, semi-legal, and not-apparently-legal population, the state of the union is stronger than ever. The purification of the citizenry has left us with an unprecedented surplus. I know many of you are ruefully wondering what we're going to do with all the crates of meat products accumulating in our ports, all the fruit rotting in the trees, all the trash accruing in our streets, all the unattended children, their diapers shat, babbling an English straight out of a 1940s Hollywood film. And I'm here to tell you this: the job before us has never been so easy. All we have to do is import people. With our kindness spread across our faces and a few bucks clutched behind our backs, we get to choose: the bait shall be our butcher shop. Gentlemen, ladies, let's not forget: successive invasions of the United States have created a favorable environment for our culture to flourish like radiata pine, burgeoning from within the souls of foreign individuals and societies. Today I'm here to make promises: we'll use our white purchasing power to import workers with university degrees so that they may exercise all the occupations that you folks would reject: street-cleaners, housekeepers, cooks, nanny-goats, drivers, security guards, mailmen, builders, secretaries, students electrified by politics so that all of you will at least have something to write about. We'll import hyper-qualified personnel and make sure they're assigned the very worst jobs. We'll corrode them from within, we'll suck out all their strength, we'll obliterate their self-esteem, we'll pay them insufficiently. They'll be looking for quite a lot of jobs, so we'll import just a few—and they'll come on ships, they'll come on planes, they'll come on buses, they'll come on foot, eager to be assessed, stock-marketed, their parts ready to be invested in shares. Any disheartened friend is a friend of ours. A defenseless enemy is obliging and affectionate. We'll only have to be vigilant in our own beds, because that's where they usually strike, dagger in hand. We'll defend ourselves: we'll contain them in special cities, where we'll furnish them with entertainment and retrograde ideas so that all of you, queridos compatriotas míos, may feel adequately liberal. These imports will be your round-the-clock friends. We'll give you the opportunity to make brown-skinned, heavy-accented buddies and thus protect your sense of self-righteousness. Our friendship is our finest weapon. We'll greet them with projectiles concealed behind our grins. This year, you'll be proud to be yourselves. You'll never notice that you were the ones who pierced their souls from within. Remember: an American citizen is always a citizen with a clean conscience.

In 1987, I have 241 speeches left to write. We met when I moved to a poor Seattle neighborhood and first entered the classroom, not knowing a word of English. I detected Selene and Mia in the back row. They were the only girls who didn't have straightened hair and nails polished the same pink as their lips. Theirs were black, their eyes shadowed cornflower blue, their hair disheveled. I took a seat nearby. I nodded and stammered as I did in Spanish. They exchanged glances and spoke to me in low voices, drowsy-eyed, moving their fists.

In 1988, I have 232 speeches left to write. One day I came home late at night from school, after languishing at Mia's house and fiddling with the instruments that belonged to her brother, the rapist. My house was empty. I could only hear the neighbor knocking on the bathroom window. I opened it, pointing a knife at him. Keeping a few steps' distance, he told me that los blancos had taken my mom when she defended the neighbors from la migra. No one had intervened on her behalf. They'd all stuck their heads in the sand, frightened by their false social security numbers and homemade papers. My mom didn't have papers, either, and they kicked me out when I went to see her at the police station. I only managed to talk with her when a long-distance operator put me through.

En el año 2018, escribí for the man with the face of an eel, the skin of an egg, eyes like an owl:

Mr. General Secretary, Madam President, distinguished delegates amid the mob, and all the rest of you. Today this country commemorates the seventeenth anniversary of the attacks that plastered the front pages of newspapers across the globe. Since then, the enemies of humanity have continued their campaign to destroy the free world. Some years ago, I sat among you all and listened to unseemly plans for the war against terror, policies that advocated for peace. But wars aren't won with peace, peace isn't the end of war. I stand before you today to reaffirm our self-esteem, both within and beyond our borders, both within and beyond our empire. As I deliver this message to you, I'm very proud to be accompanied by the generals of our militias and the leaders of the pro-weapon citizen associations that have long been a pillar of our quest for liberty: the NRA, the NMA, the NTA, the NBBA, the NNBA, the NSGA, the NKA, and the NNWA, all fighting for the right to bear and use rifles, missiles, bombs, nuclear bombs, handguns, knives, punches, and ninja stars modified to ergonomically fit the hands of Teutonic descendants on this side of the northern Atlantic.

In 1991, I have 197 speeches left to write. Selene and Mia didn't move in with me, but they often slept over at the empty house and read my poems and songs when I left to work at Bicho's bar. When winter came, we got into Selene's car and loaded it up with the instruments that belonged to Mia's brother, the rapist. A month later, we performed our first song from the stage at Bicho's. We shouted Mia's brother's name and the names of the cops who'd taken away my mother as if we were christening a bullet.

In 1992, I have 123 speeches left to write. We released our first EP, *There's a Dyke in the Pit*. My guitar roared like a chainsaw and Selene's voice barked into the microphone. Mia's epic drumming opened the final song in our concert for the press and Selene's botched Spanish thundered our cover of "Me gusta ser una zorra." From the platform, we watched the motorcyclists coming in, naked women tattooed onto their arms. They shoved at the bodies in the audience as they accumulated at our feet and jostled like livid cattle. Until my guitar smashed over the head of Mia's brother, the rapist, who now wore trashy clothes and had a swastika inked on his shoulder. That night, in jail, I wrote the song "Dead Men

Don't Rape," wanting to give strength to Mia, who was lying on the floor of the cell with a black eye and bloodied face.

En el año 2016, escribí for the man with trumpeted lips:

> I stand here today, proud of the task before us, grateful for the trust you have bestowed upon me, mindful of the misguided actions of those who have come before us and of the corrections I myself must make. I am honored, not humbled, to stand here, following the tradition of so many great men. La historia de la libertad: it is a story of flawed and fallible men, united across generations by a grand, enduring power. In these last months of the campaign, we've seen countless lies slung about by the liberal press, lies against me and the ideals for which men like myself get out of bed every morning, determined to confront the chaos permeating our society. Ideals that the seditious are intent on annihilating. I'm here to tell you that the life of a man with money, young or old, college student or president, will never be destroyed by twenty minutes of error, by a grope at the body of a woman offering herself up to him as she walks down the street. El pueblo americano ha dicho: what is a man supposed to do in the face of such beauty? This administration guarantees men's right to exhibit their impulse, their desire, the most superficial thoughts and the most profound. Hemos dicho: this administration

will defend the rights of the Tylers and the Connors, the Donalds and the Patricks. Make no mistake: we will remember their names and forget that their victims ever had one.

In 1993, we released our single "Dead Men Don't Rape." We watched women crowding against the counter, clutching quarters from the tips they'd earned mere hours before. We'd brought 200 copies. We sold them all. The next week, with rank armpits and shaggy legs, everyone chanted in chorus:

> No, my revenge is death, 'cuz you deserve the best
> And I'm not turned on by your masculinity
> Dead men don't rape.
> I don't have pity, not a single tear
> For those who get joy from women's fear.

As she sang, Selene stared into the eyes of Mia's brother, the rapist:

> I'd rather get a gun and just blow you away
> Then you'll learn firsthand: dead men don't rape.

In 1994, I still have many speeches left to write for a man who'd sooner leave me speechless. I got a call. Selene's voice was hoarser than usual. They'd finally found Mia. She hadn't been tripping, as she often did. She hadn't enjoyed it. They'd found her body tortured and wound-ravaged. Her face expressed pain. Mia's brother was at large and they'd only managed to find one of his friends, tying him to a chair in the basement. We left him dying in the hospital. The pain I felt the night of Mia's funeral instantly multiplied the next day, when I learned that Selene had been in a car accident. In search of Mia's brother, the rapist, her car had been pushed off the road by motorcyclists whose wheels left skid marks on the pavement.

This story is dedicated to Mia Zapata, raped and murdered in 1993, and to Susana Chávez, victim of a similar crime in 2011. Este cuento no está terminado. Esta venganza is to be continued.

Invocation

Cars on Fire

People always said heat waves weren't what they used to be. Every morning the humidity crawled in from the swampy gardens, seeping through the mosquito nets and into the mattress. The bedroom's discomfort would ignite and he'd have to put it out with the hose from the house next door. Just before waking, his dreams would turn vivid and resume whatever had happened the night before. This-guy—symptom, loner, trudger—thinks mornings are strange, out of place.

As he descends the stairs, he's met with the occupations his father used to threaten him with, like a line-up of ghosts: this-beggar reading tarot cards on a bench in the square. This-numbskull selling water bottles on the corner of Atlantic and Nostrand. This-busybody reading a book, sprawled out on the sidewalk, covered with that blanket that this-guy, this-animal, stepped on yesterday as he made his way home from work on East 11th. This-guy stumbling, feeling the city's pavement under his back. *Dirty streets scorching in the sun.*

The concrete boils. He sees it in the celestial wakes that rise up from the asphalt and the smell emanating from the piss-puddles trailed by the garbage trucks as they cut across the city with their sculpted workers on board. The sidewalks are vaguely sticky. The block-dwellers now occupy their front steps. Some have brought out chairs and fan themselves with the pages of half-read newspapers. Others water plants to refresh them, and also the moss that reaches like a jungle up through the fence and the red brick walls. He closes the gate behind him, a heavy backpack slung over his shoulder. He seems to be hearing his father's recriminations, his practical voice. This-guy—dog, gringo, milksop—can't bear it.

The street is silent for a moment before the cicadas chime in again. They've been complaining for months now. The interjected rip-rip sound of the broom was only an interlude: a bus, the beeps of construction trucks in reverse as they drill into wet ears and houses with renovated façades and wealthier inhabitants. Meanwhile, the shouts of people seeking shade beneath the elms, bare feet, shorts clinging to ass-cracks, pants hanging from hips, sleeveless T-shirts, muscled chests abandoning their shirts atop their bicycle seats, clothes translucent with sweat, thick, braided hair gathered as far away as possible from their bodies, which cook in the sun. No one is spared.

This-guy—demented, transcendental—opens the car door and slams into the dense smell of old things. He is forced to lower the windows and confirm, circling the car, that nothing has come loose during the night. Not a single piece, right, Dad? The once-gleaming leather seats, now looking more like armadillo scales, start to air out. And as soon as he can bear touching his bare legs to the grayish surface, he starts the ignition, hiding his face a little. A shiver of shame glints through him. Maybe no one would notice, huh, Dad? The smell of gasoline fills the car. He grunts. Almost a miracle that the car starts at all, said the mechanic who'd fixed the dent just after he bought the car directly from its twenty-sixth owner, the one who offered to repair the mark, mend the *o* around the inverted *y* decorating the chassis, remove the brown stickiness slicked across it, replace the lost tire and the missing wood panels, paint over the scratches keyed onto it (who knows where or in what neighborhood) by some passer-by who'd glanced at the '79 Mercedes and seen a millionaire to be despised. Who'd seen a proud family man, a father like his own, with children and purchases filling the trunk where this-guy, reneging on his father's designs, now keeps a blanket and an orange traffic cone in case he gets stuck somewhere. This mirror, this metal. What had happened with the car had also happened with the father: reneging on the son's designs, he had departed forever in a car like this car, perhaps the very same. Both car and father, then, had left him with a vague memory of a snazzy suburb in a city booming with the automotive industry. *Just watch out. Tomorrow it might be you.*

He focuses on the maneuver. It takes half an hour just to move it to the other side of the road. He doesn't look at anyone, although he notes their presence on the stoops and sidewalks. A blue tide surges from the hot exhaust pipe and it makes children cough, old men curse, and youths cover their mouths in the attic of the house next door. This-guy—violent, crease-browed—pretends he doesn't hear them. He's dedicating his own internal insults to the father he barely knew. Right?

It's going to explode. Outside the car's grimy windows, he confirms, the world looks even hazier and more toxic. *Doan yu theenk?* He struggled to fix his eyes on the origin of the hoarse, forced voice. A body seated on the stoop of the house next door. One of its eyes obscured by its hair, the other half-closed and streaked with makeup melted in the heat. *I don't think so.* The colors reappear along the road. The woman sitting on the stoop, the notebook-neighbor, wipes the sweat from her hand on the cut-off denim taut against her thigh and tucks her piled-up books under her arm when she gets to her feet and climbs the stairs. Her fingers are stained with ink. *Have you taken it to the shop? Cars aren't supposed to give off blue smoke,* she coughs. Who, beneath this heavy sun, could possibly know more about cars than this-guy—foppish, pinched. His father, perhaps.

At a table in the library, he rereads a novel about an urban project that transforms a dilapidated industrial city into a model city occupied by artists. According to the narrator's plan, each artist would be assigned a bedroom and studio in the old buildings, refurbished with a rich state's cash, as befitting their experience and résumé. Artists would come to this model city wearing only the clothes on their backs and would be obliged to construct everything else. In their role, which would fall somewhere between creation and unemployment, the artists would receive paltry salaries until they managed to establish themselves. He's flooded with laughter as he reads. A real man is a working man, right, Dad? He makes a note on his computer: after the successive failures of the automotive industry, the U.S. can be interpreted as a model of failed hyper-industrialization, with an income equality typical of poor countries. A country that belongs to two worlds, both colonial and imperial. Does the novel suggest that there's something respectable about being unemployed? He stops typing at the memory of a termination letter, an empty job, a suburban garage with no car in it.

When he gets home, various neighbors are chatting from their front porches, calling over their gates. Asked about his writing, this-guy offers a vague answer, determined to obscure his doubts as to whether two years of solitary interpretative work on Detroit's automotive industry could make any sense to anyone other than himself. They inform him that the neighbor is also writing her doctoral dissertation. Then, gesturing across the street, they mention that the couple who recently moved into #1454 are writers, too, and swimming in money. They look at the dark façade, suddenly more ornate under the construction tarps than anyone had ever noticed. The neighborhood is, then, the model city. Isn't it? Its small quarters and floor-divisions serve only to lodge the pencil-artists who need nothing more than a desk and a window. This-guy—corrosive, vegetal—gives a final glance at the moving van before saying goodbye and going in.

He peers attentively into the screen. Perhaps the true protagonists of Lelouch's 1966 film *Un homme et une femme* are not in fact the characters played by Anouk Aimée and Jean-Louis Trintignant, but rather the car, its speed, the rain. They're damaged souls. A Formula 1 driver races along French highways and into the arms of the woman he's been romancing. Both are recently widowed. Her husband had worked as a stunt double and was killed filming a car sequence. His wife, increasingly distressed every time he took the wheel, had committed suicide. Condemned to repeat their trauma, much of the film involves the racecar driver traversing the distance and a harsh atmosphere evolving between him and his new love. Death inhabits the past. Death approaches with its foot on the gas. The racecar driver, however, reaches his destination in his super-sports car—the latest model Alfa Romeo—that will plunge off a cliff at the toss of a stone.

At night, this-guy, this lost soul, this animal in heat, dreams he is carrying on a conversation with his neighbor in which she argues that writing a dissertation could become a method of automatic writing, as practiced by the surrealists and other artists obsessed with the subconscious, if it could access the part of the subconscious that retains empty forms over and over again. In the dream, the neighbor explains her theory by sketching a brain with blue pen. This-guy feels the pressure against his temples. Instead of unleashing the imagination, her hoarse voice continues, you enter a place full of *lugares comunes*. The drawing is now a turban heaped with flowers, pineapples, other fruits, the one Carmen Miranda wore in the movie about Rio de Janeiro, or about Havana, or about any place with dark skin, red lips, a flat belly, and a Latin accent, like the neighbor's. The dream features young women who have been trained to say, in English, *Americans always say my hat is high*.

He wakes with a headache. When he sees the neighbor eating a banana, this-guy—small, drowsy with heat and insomnia—thinks of her strong accent. In Detroit it was cars. In Brazil, bananas and women. Don't you think something interesting could be written about this? *Gud moarning*. That evening, she would write a chapter about the guy who would speak to her in a distant dream. Carmen Miranda was catapulted to fame in a dress characteristic of northern Brazil. Her physique was convenient: fair skin, almond-shaped eyes, perfect smile, the perfect banana *da terra*. *The lady with the tutti frutti hat*. Despite her millions, Carmen Miranda tried to escape the stereotype. But, as usual, the pact wasn't quite so easily broken. World War Two suppressed the national appetite for exoticism, replacing this business with the white-skinned arms trade.

He pauses beside the window of the rattletrap. This-guy—docile, eternal son—keeps his eyes on the ground. The battered bumper. The yellow paint like a wayside shrine from another era. The blue blankets disheveled in the trunk, expelling a smell of forest and pasture. *This shit's gonna explode.* The hot coffee searing his tongue, but not as hot as his neighbor's attic, where she swims in books and movies. Earbuds always in her ears. A little notebook where she writes things down.

The conversation gets off to a vague start. This-guy—very quiet in the corner—fucking hates cars. He's going to put this personal anecdote in the first pages of the introduction. He was born the same year Saddam Hussein received the keys to the city of Detroit. His father worked in one of the offices on the outskirts. He earned good money until he fell prey to a mass layoff. The house in the suburbs started to come apart at the seams with a despondent father inside it. *Don't you believe me?* His voice a thin thread. This-guy barely remembers him except for the '79 car he bought in hopes of it being the one that once belonged to his father, repairing it in hopes of repairing his memory of his father. This-guy—stereotypical, automatic—would write the very best academic paper.

The fountain-pen-resting-on-the-marble-table-neighbor, the coffee-cup-neighbor, tells him she's writing about people who travel by plane. One woman, pen in hand, took a flight to keep from disappearing like the people in her novels. A few years before, she'd shattered a champagne glass in her hands after feeling humiliated by an award she hadn't received: it had been promised to her, they were cooking it up. *But she was never much of a cook, you know?* Then she'd fired a gun she always carried around in one of her patent leather purses, a gun with a crystal handle that she fixed on an old boyfriend she hadn't seen in a decade. She came to *Nu Yoark* in 1944, this Bombal woman. She changed her hairstyle and avoided looking at herself in the mirror because it called her Luisa and it called her María. She only allowed people to take photos of her in places where she'd already located a small glass within her field of vision. It contained, according to her, a small dram of her health. She picked up a pen and got married. What else could she do with that exquisite education and the absent mother she bore like a transparent, ghostly body? Maybe in California, or here in New York, her pen could set the limits she'd so struggled to describe, constantly repeating the word Luisa, the word María from afar. She could even marry a count who would give her a noble daughter. She could even write a screenplay that the count would sell. But in the end, she just went back to Chile, without a pen and with various broken glasses.

This-guy—scrawny, foul smelling—and the coffee-cup-carrying-neighbor now make their way toward the art gallery. As a teenager, this-guy, this piece of garbage, spent lots of time with his friends in abandoned suburban houses, spray-painting and sometimes destroying them with machetes and fists, music and beer. His drawings always depicted car parts, just like the Peruvian artist who had part of a car in half his studio. When this-guy tells the coffee-cup-neighbor and the car-parts-artist that he writes about the automotive industry and unions in Detroit, the paintings-man tells him that his agent had bought an entire neighborhood there. To found an artist's residency. Every house cost him a dollar and he pays the property taxes in artworks.

This-guy—singular, enchained—walks around the gallery, observing the pieces on the shelves. It's as if he were looking through his father's eyes. This-guy zipping up his pants in the bathroom, brushing a hand across his face in the mirror, brown socks. Taking out the trash, a line of black garbage bags accumulating on the sidewalk in front of identical houses painted different colors. Doing the numbers with a five-dollar calculator, his fingers laced in his black curls, sweaty and slick. Sitting on the subway with half a cheek turned outward, about to get up at any moment. Dialing an always-busy phone number and eventually leaving a hesitant message. Later, scraping shit from a shoe, wondering what the fuck he's doing at 11 P.M. when the neighbors greet him and his shoe is plastered in shit. Spying on the neighbor on the stairs of the house next door from his own window, imagining her: the neighbor squeezing toothpaste onto a toothbrush, the neighbor walking down the street, the neighbor stopping in front of a stained-glass window, sitting down after pulling out several boxes of books. This-guy drinking coffee in the middle of summer, reading on the subway, in the house of the neighbor who has no family in this country. And this-guy, who does he think he is?

At nearly a hundred degrees Fahrenheit, the metal seems alive. And so this-guy, this good-for-nothing, leaves it stranded in the middle of the road again. The rolled-down windows and uttered insults make him lower his eyes. His white muscles try to move it a few centimeters toward the sidewalk. Isn't that better, Dad? The men who linger in the street every day, the men this popinjay doesn't so much as wave at, stare at him from a distance without altering their day's affairs, their impalpable commerce. The strength of such arms would move this car like a feather. Library body, he hears like a whisper. *It was bound to happen.* The tow truck guy sits for several minutes in the driver's seat, texting, despite the horns blasting on both sides of Dean Street. This-guy—chicken-skin—is getting anxious, tormented by the pages he's stopped writing. *Maybe it's time to sell it.* The sentence hits him with a drop of acrid sweat. The hoarse voice reads his mind. The neighbor appears with her short-shorts, skinny legs, belly bared, damp shirt, bag on her shoulder, an expression somewhere between irony and concern. *It was bound to happen.*

They watch the operation in silence. *In Chile, we could get in with him or go in your car.* They stop a green cab. This-guy opens the door for her and immediately regrets it a little, is a little ashamed of such chivalry. Don't you think? The neighbor watches him count his bills and warily chews her gum. Her gaze shifts as she maybe wonders why she offered to come along and whether she can still get out before things get weird. This-guy—foggy, firm—tells her he can't sell it, no one would buy it anymore. It was never expensive, he clarifies at the jobless neighbor's incredulous look. Typical. Look at this-guy. In Detroit, buying a German car was read as an act of defiance. This model has electric windows, a sunroof, air-conditioning, interlayered windshields, a collapsible steering column, central locking, an electric mirror on the driver's side, automatic transmission.

This-guy—who doesn't take his eyes from the driver in front of him—talks incessantly the entire way, unsure whether the sweaty-skinned neighbor is listening. The inverted-*y* turbo diesel model appeared in 1979, a novelty for this kind of family car. Its six-cylinder 0M167 engine has a 125-horsepower capacity, like this one, exceeding 320 kilometers per hour on test drives. The model, which can accommodate a stroller, was designed for suburban life and fantasies of far-off travel. At 179 centimeters wide and 149 centimeters high, it leaves a lot of space for its seven possible passengers. The roof rack measures a little over one square meter. The body is steel and the fuel tank is located above the rear axle. Its design ensures the very highest safety standards, right, Dad? It absorbs shocks and enables maximum visibility in all directions. It saves the lives of young bourgeois families, offering a soft-close mechanism with child-proofable pin locks on the doors and panoramic windows. The broad bumpers, embellished with elastic material and wide rubber edges, complete the design. The glory of days past. *So what was your father like?*

The heat falls onto them and sears their skin. The notebook-neighbor shields herself with a copy of *El Especialito* that she'd pulled from the newspaper dispenser on the corner. Looking out onto the street, she lets the flitting heat-stunned bugs alight on her arms. Even smashing them would be too much work. This-guy—he who seeks the remnants of his manliness—thinks as he closes his wallet that he should probably shoo them away, shouldn't he, Dad? What, if not, are the chances of a man forever shattered by a father's absence? This-guy thinks of Roberta, who was traveling around Denmark the last time they spoke. *I didn't know we'd come all the way to Jersey City.* The neighbor's forced, almost sleepy voice seeps out of the old radio that was the humidity itself. *This is Kennedy Boulevard. This transplanted underdevelopment that our families flaunt. Conspicuous, incongruous.* This-guy—dazed—moves his jaw from side to side as he always does when he doesn't know what to say. They walk from the bus to the ferry and lick red and blue shaved ices, like the flags of France, Texas, and Chile, with the little choo-choo-train chugging along in the poetry of Lourdes Casal, transformed into *una revolucionaria* on Kennedy Boulevard. Since she was a distinguished diplomat and intellectual, no one dared to say lesbian. Ensconced at home or at the office, some swore on their loved ones' graves that they'd met the boyfriend who'd broken her heart and left her this way: sort of masculine, devoted to the life of the mind. She came here as a Cuban, a rosary around her neck. She went back black. The *Yuneited Esteits*, the need to become a revolution. *I carry this marginality, immune to all turning back.*

At the entrance to the public library, this-guy—he of the millenary void—has lost all desire to write. He sits and promptly falls asleep. When he opens his eyes, the keyboard has marked its squares into his cheek, so crisply inserted that it hurts to pull away. Through the window of the library, he sees Kowalski's tight pants, the ones he's been dreaming of these past few nights. The small body is surrounded by snow, getting into a white car, and this-guy, who knows nothing, realizes it's November. According to the photos he's pulled from various abandoned boxes, his father looked nothing like Barry Newman. His father looked taller, and only in one photograph was he wearing such tight pants. *Vanishing Point* came to theaters in 1971. His father must have been in Los Angeles, bound for Detroit, or maybe even in Mexico City. It meant something, didn't it, Dad, that the film was showing in theaters while his own slender body and prominent nose were getting into a car and driving around the U.S., as he'd previously done in who knows what border town of a communist country later divided in the '90s. It must have seemed like quite an adventure, right? Watching TV and staring at the screens of wherever you were from.

On a beat-up VHS, this-guy—invertebrate, practically Iberian—watches the movie again. Kowalski's trip from Colorado to California in record time, sleepless and hyped up on speed, is intercut with various flashbacks informing us that he is a Vietnam veteran, an ex-cop discharged for reporting his partner's perpetration of sexual abuse, an ex-motorcycle racer, an ex-Formula 1 driver no one remembers, and the lover of an ethereal woman who is no longer there. The melancholy, ethical, suicidal masculinity of Kowalski, who has no first name, never sleeps. The women are all one woman or they're the sweet sun on the horizon, the fantasy of death. The lonely man in the desert. With his car. On fire.

In the first scene of *Vanishing Point*, the white Dodge Challenger—Challenger could easily be the character's first name; come to think of it, the father's—hurtles down the highway at top speed, such that man and car simultaneously embody Renaissance and Futurist ideals. The final scene repeats this to the death. The consciousness of an evaporating country.

The final collision could also be interpreted as the purest, simplest form of propaganda. During the years prior to the film's premiere, numerous complaints were filed regarding faulty car-manufacturing at the Ford and General Motors plants in Detroit, including the most popular and exclusive models. Sales dropped by 93%. The fact that an expert driver like Kowalski crashes of his own volition into earthly bulldozers shifts blame from the industry, engulfed by confrontations with unions and popular movements, to the client—creating, in the process, the fantasy of heroism that outlives anyone who dies at the wheel.

I'd check the crash reports if I were you. When this-guy tells the whole story to the neighbor, who is buying a cup of coffee at the deli on the corner of their block, she tells him that the screenplay was written by Guillermo Cabrera Infante. *There can't be too many cars like that one.* Can there? This-guy, who doesn't know exactly who she's talking about, mumbles something about the screenplay. The neighbor, not taking this-guy—strapped, fetishistic, calculating—very seriously, smiling slightly in her third-floor apartment, the attic of a house with a mattress on the floor, hands him a copy of *Tres Tristes Tigres* and tells him that the screenplay is archived at a nearby university.

And what you write is suddenly real. The ink-stain-on-the-face-neighbor closes her fingerless gloves around another steaming cup of coffee and glances up, sheathed in a black wool hat, at the thirty-fourth floor of the building on Mercer Street. The thing is that writing can never be automatic enough, because the writer always has to come back, pick up the pen, get hold of a body to print things onto the surface. She looks at him steadily. *So I can't have been the one who said that in your dream. Pero qué sucede* if you don't have a body when you come back, she says to this-guy who was a family man in last night's dream.

The full-bag-of-books-neighbor is standing on Mercer St. before her writing day at the library. Ana Mendieta left her country in a fish tank. She was put there when she was twelve years old. From the other side, she saw her father, the one who kept the guns, the one who went to jail, saying goodbye to her. She kissed the Miami ground when she got off the plane, as she'd seen a pope do before 1959. She turned from a messiah into a child in a refugee camp, a house in Iowa, an orphanage. From family to family, her strong Cuban accent was perceived as a mark of inferiority. She used her body as a transformative entity. So, too, the language she shared with her mother and her *mama*. Her body left landmarks in galleries, in pits she dug in fields, in museums in Britain, Rome, Berlin. On city streets, in the voices of New York, in photographs, in tracts of land outside Havana, was a silhouette of Ana Mendieta's body. A silhouette was left when she fell from the thirty-fourth floor, naked, as in her performances. ¿Un cuerpo que escribe su futuro? *There's always an unlaid stone in the ground.*

The back-pain-neighbor sneezes and covers the viscous liquid that her nose expels. She stays in position, tissue at her face, as if counting the seconds it took Mendieta to hit the ground. *Lo que debe haber sido.* This-guy knows she's murmuring in her most intimate language, the one she speaks deepest inside herself. It sounds to this-guy like a lament for who knows what. Walking, taking little sips from her coffee, the neighbor tells him that she's looking for work. This-guy—he of the raised eyebrow—doesn't understand what this has to do with the Cuban artist's suicide. What happens in the model city isn't a real job, right, Dad? Sometimes people who catch sight of him on the street think he does something feminine, like keep a diary. When they part ways, he sees it's snowing and realizes he never asked her where the jobs she's looking for are located.

The street is lit by burgeonings of snow. It falls from the trees. It falls from the rooftops. It falls, like this-guy's gaze on the third floor. The notebook-neighbor now has a suitcase she takes out for a walk several times that month. He doesn't see her for days. The frigid mattress, the solitary nights—they intersect with the stripped tree branches tossed by wind like a falling, falling angel. At night, looking out the window from the corner of his eye, his drowsy eye, this-guy—mute, blank—confuses the snow with people walking down the middle of the road. Bodies are unrecognizable under coats, parkas, hats, boots, gloves, balaclavas. The snow illuminates the street, casting shadows where there used to be none. They file along after the last big snowfall as if on a movie set, orderly, one a night, while this-guy shovels snow around three in the morning without a single light on. One night he sees a big man with a child in his arms. They're wearing the same garments, like they're the same person on different planes. The next night he sees two people walking side by side, a man and a woman. Every so often the woman slips, moving awkwardly in a way he recognizes at once. Roberta. Holding the hand of another man whose face he doesn't see. He doesn't stop, just tells her it's unwise to walk across the layer of snow that sifts between them. When he wakes, he sees that the storm has passed and the snow has heaped up on cars, in the streets. The night allows him to make out a single silhouette, a slight body dragging along a suitcase. He of the shovel-in-hand hurries to help, but he hears a car engine behind him, a shuddering accelerator. When he turns around, this-guy, blinded by the light, wakes up.

This-guy—ricocheting about his life—opens the door. He's suddenly met with the smell of spring. He's handed a package addressed to a woman who lives in the house next door, but he doesn't recognize the name. It's heavy and he doesn't know what to do with it. He looks skyward and decides it isn't yet time to plant flowers, or is it?, but give this-guy any excuse to spend time outside, in the fresh air, without waiting for Roberta to call. This-guy, snuffling, cleans his flowerpot stand and Gary's from the second floor. The inky-fingered neighbor leans against the gate and speaks in Spanish with the neighbor from #1433. This-guy—he of the sidelong glance—thinks they're talking about him and he becomes that-guy, he of the clumsy body. The coffee-cup neighbor waves at him and gestures toward the street, her lips pursed like a duck beak. It's the car that belongs to the new people who recently moved in next to the husky-voiced neighbor—duplex doors, thin walls.

They're getting out of a Mercedes 300 Coupe that's the same color as his, sort of a creamy coffee color, and certainly the same model year as the car that belongs to the guy looking for his father. They keep it in perfect condition and without the ridiculous rear that distinguishes his own. *Hi there.* The Spanish-speaking women have fallen silent. Pretty weird, huh, Dad? Two nearly identical cars have ended up end-to-end right in front of the neighbor's house. *We got you covered.*

Do you know them? The voice emerges from the unsteady body climbing the stairs. They look out from the neighbor's attic window. The dissertation-neighbor opens the three windows that the sunlight and a faint heat come through. She hasn't let go of the plastic flowerpot holder. *Weird, isn't it?* This-guy's voice—dirt-stained—comes out of him from somewhere else, because he knows that the image will slip into his dreams tonight. *I don't know them.* Right, Dad? How many cars like that one came in through the eastern border in '79? They sift in the soil a little at a time, carefully settling the wildflower seeds in place. This-guy knows that the red-pencil-neighbor could do this by herself, but he already spends so many hours of the day writing alone that this-guy—he who assesses with a clinical eye—sees the jumbled books as a symbol of the mental chaos that inhabits his room, like hers. Unemployment starts to strain through the cracks of the model city.

From the armchair where he observes this undertaking and listens to the morbid bolero, he reaches out a hand through the living room until he can touch the neighbor's bare thigh. He hesitates for a moment when he sees his own fingernails caked with dirt and grime, but those things only matter in dreams, right, Dad? As his hand finds its way, he imagines an entire life with her, the book-discarded-on-the-windowsill-neighbor: this-guy waking in a bed like her bed, this-guy leaving a house like hers in the morning, looking out a window like hers, walking down the stairs in another house, almost hers, kissing the naked air from below as if the above were his. A hand on his shoulder shakes him awake. This jolt, this earth. Hoarsely, she introduces him to the people standing before him. So forever out of place—the place of the unemployed, he seems to hear his father say—that he feels he should go.

Misfortune stops inside the car. This-guy—stranger to himself—presses on the gas as he starts to hear the neighbor's throaty voice on the phone, and this body starts to miss her nearness. At some point the things they're writing about bump into each other. 1896: they interrupt each other. The same year of the first film screenings in the whole world, the same year when the first horseless carriage embarks down the street. *No, 1920, sometime around then.* Not long before, the Ford automobile plant had settled in on the outskirts of Santiago. Sales weren't good. The U.S. ambassador, seated in the cold, neoclassical office he'd decorated baroquely, lest he forget where he came from, met with some local businessmen to foment the projection of American films. The public, the people, sensed something that made them grit their teeth. Now bearing sums of money allocated for trips to the city-that-never-sleeps, the businessmen left, slightly drunk, to find the car that would take them from the park to the ministry. Availing himself of the recently installed telephone lines, the ambassador informed some city, some office, and some ear full of hair gel that the deciding thumb had shifted upward. In the ensuing years, American films flooded theaters, their elegant halls newly fumigated to get rid of the fleas—a plague of them had inundated the southern city that very year. Soon, the very same people who had gone to work that morning at the Ford plant would buy cocktails at the movie theater bar, dressed in the same short-hemmed suits as the actors moving around onscreen. They'd drive cars like the high-heels-and-slit-skirt car and clog traffic along the *alamedas*. The twenty-first century: the advent of horror.

This-guy—disoriented, slightly aroused by the brush of the hoarse voice—decides not to hear the final comment, as he's learned by now to identify certain minor provocations from the pencil-and-empty-wallet neighbor. He looks for a parking spot and decides to stop waiting for Roberta.

Misfortune accelerates inside the car. This-guy works to keep her on the line. Henry Ford was the only American to garner a favorable mention in *Mein Kampf.* It would seem that the dictator's admiration for the businessman earned him Nazi Germany's highest honors: a prize measured in money, parties, women, a gold plaque, and a role overseeing the provision of the productive model through which Hitler would practice his genocide.

There's a silence on the line, as if a wall had suddenly gone up between this-guy and the fountain-pen-neighbor. He hesitates in the street.

When he rings the bell, he doesn't yet know that he's attending a goodbye party. This-guy—adamantine, cruel—has visualized a full, intimate evening. By then, he feels the lack of nothing more acutely than the presence of the inky-fingered neighbor. When he goes up, however, lots of people are there. He loses count before greeting anyone. Alcohol stalks him. How many are there, Dad? Suddenly the room empties out and leaves only five, who sit down to eat. The flowers they'd planted together have blossomed. The red spreads through the house and into the neighbor's springy dress. This-guy—he of the unstormy desire—notes that she's cut her hair, painted her nails, and seems happier than ever before. She clearly has, too, a close relationship with every one of the other three men who face him at the table, speaking English with heavy and occasionally incomprehensible accents. The first seems curiously at home there: her kisses hound him. The second exudes an excessive familiarity with the neighbor, a rapport possible only with someone you live with. The third has a tactile relationship with the neighbor: their fingers are tenderly laced together. He addresses this-guy—he of the closed mouth, he who looks inward—and asks about his work. He imagines, through his father's eyes, what he might say: a population graphic illustrating the growth of Detroit, twenty-five times its size in under twenty years, photographs of the Ford Co. assembly line, the city's majestically abandoned buildings. The trouble began just a few years after the boom. In the 1930s, the crisis prompted mass lay-offs and plummeting salaries forced immigrants and citizens to see their lives from a new perspective. This abandonment, this road. The industry recovered by manufacturing tanks and war vehicles. Malcolm X was among the hundreds, thousands, working in the factories. Union leaders were crushed, beaten, spit at, burned, and fired. In the late '50s, Detroit's population dropped by 25%. The downtown area, which had once represented the long-dreamed empire, was desolate. Around it were hundreds of unemployed people, poor people, beggars. Motor City, Murder City.

He could explain so many other things, too. Right, Dad? 1971, the job at Chrysler; 1973, the oil crisis; 1979, debt; 1982, a letter of dismissal; 1984, an empty garage. Instead of that, with the coffee-smell wafting in from the kitchen, the radio thrums "Motor City is Burning."

Birdsong invades his room through the open window. A bird has perched on a cable within his field of vision. He watches it warble. It has an extraordinary vocal range, imitating, with notable precision, the calls of the thrush, the robin, the hen harrier, and several others whose names he doesn't know.

He wonders whether the bird sings with a particular intention, or if it's rehearsing, or if it's maybe enjoying the very act of imitation, using the patios between the houses and buildings as a sounding board.

In a state of neither wakefulness nor sleep, he assesses the kilometers separating his body from the foot of the bed, which seems to move like an oceanic horizon as he crosses from one shore to the other uncertain one. In response to this thought, the sweat accumulated on his neck, inner thighs, and armpits becomes a sea. He floats and sinks.

He walks the eleven blocks to where he'd parked his car the night before. He opens the door, places his heavy backpack inside, and inspects it twice, making sure everything is as he left it. He starts the engine, revs it hard, and feels a new vibration underfoot, something superimposed over the layer of loose metal. He turns it off and starts it up again, pressing on the accelerator with all his strength. A slight scent of gas seeps into the car, as if the heat from the subsoil were about to transform it into fire. He guides it along, slowly, among the other vehicles seeking out a parking space at that hour, hoping to avoid a fine from the garbage truck. It's unusual for him to find a spot right in front of his house, right beside the new neighbors' identical vehicle. They greet him coldly as they settle their sleepy daughter into her seat. Only then does he see two enormous red suitcases and two small ones, each sporting a gaudy luggage tag, on the inky-fingered neighbor's front steps. The name on the tag is the same as the one on the package he received months ago and kept without knowing exactly who it was for. He's startled to realize that its owner was his neighbor coming down the stairs. They'd never asked each other's names. How did they address each other, then? No need, they barely knew each other at all. The neighbor greets him as if for the first time. They shake hands like perfect strangers. He tells her he has a package for her, but the neighbor says it doesn't matter anymore, that it must be the potting soil. That she doesn't need it anymore because she's moving out. She asks him to give her keys to the landlord, who hasn't gotten back to her. Maybe he's sleeping on the first floor. She's moving. Where to?

In the car, on the way to the airport, this-guy—fractured soul, irreparable solitude—talks with the books-in-the-backpack neighbor. Like perfect strangers, estranged from each other, they talk about the nice weather in California, that she'll be able to speak Spanish there with pretty much anyone, that she'll probably forget her English altogether. The writer, who looks out at the industrial landscapes of Ridgewood and Jamaica, tells him she'd learned English and Spanish almost simultaneously at a school where she was taught to think she belonged somewhere else. She now struggles to believe how she felt her lifelong ailments leaving her as soon as she reached this country—how she'd recognized herself, recognized her brother, so much like her, in the passer-by getting off the subway, in the clerk at the Verizon store, in the people leaving buildings on Wall Street, in the bodies drinking whiskey in Bowery bars. In the list of surnames she sang, there were Spanish names, their creole deformations, their Arab heritage, but nothing to indicate any affiliation with the dwellers of Russian, Polish, or Czech neighborhoods she could walk through undetected. But some things can't be helped. A last name with a diacritical mark. The color of her eyes. A certain intolerance to cold. Impossible to shake off *el sur.* At the same time, a seed was growing. How could she identify so absolutely with people so quick to kill anyone else? Now she was on a new quest. *Al ni aquí ni allá.* To be from nowhere other than wherever this notebook and this pencil happened to be. Like the other women who got on a plane.

The hug with which this-guy—he of the achy ear—bids farewell to the unknown woman imprints itself into his body along with a sentence that punctures him persistently as he drives home: if only this obsession with one's roots actually accomplished anything. The night before, Roberta had finally told him she was coming back, having found the archives full of nothing but empty boxes and folders of discarded papers. Her money was running out, too. Ro-ber-ta: that name was moving away from him, replaced by the body that this-guy—embittered, self-flagellating—has just left and which has become part of his own, although he doesn't know how or why. The gas pedal falters and stops responding at a red light. The honking will start any moment now. He's in the middle of Eastern Parkway, in the lane designated for left-hand turns. The car won't start. It just emits that strange vibration, stronger now, every time he turns the key in the ignition, and the pleasant smell of gasoline fills the air. This-guy, who knows more about his car than anyone, Dad, lifts the orange cone out of the trunk and sets it down about five feet away. The shouts and honks fall silent when he opens the hood. Blue smoke overtakes everything, boiling the battery, boiling the pipes and metal, dissolving the rubber of the tires, melting the inside of the car. This-guy—he of the languid body and the living soul—crosses the street. From the corner of his eye, he sees that the open-doored car is engulfed in flames, and he leaves it behind at last.

The Animal Mosaic

It was the eve of the national festivities. In front of the house across the street, a fifteen-year-old boy, tall and lanky, extended his arm up toward the dense trees with the solemnity of someone who wasn't alone. He fired the first shot. The stars flashed in through the branches and scattered singed foliage. You could hear the songs of birds sleeping huddled against each other. Nests dropped down into the night. The second star lit the darkness and startled syrinxes loosed their warnings. Terrified, dozens of open wings invaded the block. The fifteen-year-old boy and I were the only humans there. My eyes found his from where I stood on the opposite sidewalk. He felt ashamed to see the third star reflected in my eyes. But his arm, lifted at a visionary angle, could only anticipate animal death. Night and silence fell once more. We both listened closely. When the boy went back into his house, nothing but me and the memory of the invasion were left outside, bearing witness to the dark and what would later come to pass on a staircase on Dean Street.

Those were the birds. A feather on every shard of stone.

The fifteen-year-old dreamed of rats that night. The week

before, someone had shown him a video about ordinary people from all over this vast territory called the state of the union. The people fondly stroked their rats. The images made him feel the stirring of an unknown tenderness toward the dirty animals that scrabbled in the trash behind the building on the corner of Kingston Avenue and stumbled food-drunk through the streets.

The deepest dimensions of the animal self exist not at the level of the individual but as part of the collective group mind of the entire species, and that higher level is not a duality lesson per se.

The rats in the video weren't rank or diseased. They scaled human legs. People bathed them and let their pets lick them with their mustached mouths. Something prompted him to close the window on his cell phone, something that pierced his retina and lodged itself in his body like a tremor. The feeling hounded him for weeks and forced him to tighten his sneakers hard around his ankles before he left the house.

He woke from those dreams with an unease that warped his vision and his hearing. Sometimes he confused the outside sounds with his mother's voice.

Those were the rats. A footprint on every stone.

A few weeks prior, Kuan had cut, sewn, drawn, printed, and stuffed some cushions bearing the images of cats culled from a sketchbook. When Kuan took them to sell outside after school, the fifteen-year-old decided they didn't match the stoic tone of his bedroom, constrained as he was by his meager allowance and his own minimal penchant for work of any kind.

Hundreds of these beings have manifested in full avatar mastery.

In the middle of the night, after spending several hours engrossed in his phone, he turned his bedroom inside out in search of any cash he might have lost among his notebooks. Loose coins scattered onto the bed. He was jolted awake by his mother shrilling about the mess, demanding to know if he intended to buy more of that marijuana again. He shut the front door with a shrug, as if deciding not to give any of it another thought, and he walked along the sidewalk, kicking at a trail of gnawed chicken bones. Later that same day, Kuan surprised him by holding out a bag with the last cushion inside, the one nobody had bought. The fifteen-year-old stared at the bag for a long time, half-smiling as his friends jeered. He tucked it carefully into his backpack so it wouldn't raise any suspicions at home.

He got into bed, pulled out the cushion, and placed it on top of his pillow. The cat print was an effigy. She looked straight ahead with a blanket around her shoulders. Her right paw rested on her hip, her left hand dangling a rat by the tail. The rat had Xs for eyes. The boy put on his headphones and shifted his head on Kuan's cushion.

The leanness and the muscles under the red shirt.

A shiver darted down his back when he turned off the light.

After a few minutes, he flung the cushion to the floor.

The mosaic will go on the western wall of the temple. Use the chisel and hammer to break up the pieces.

His eyes were already open when his mother came in to wake him. He couldn't shake the images of the suited men and women who'd gathered at his house the night before and tried to coax him back to the temple. They lit candles, burned incense and herbs. They filled his house with smoke and pulled off his T-shirt and slathered his torso with pungent oils. His lungs ached and his skin stung. The ritual had unleashed a fever he still felt the following morning.

When a human forms a personality fragmentation-meld with a Felidae or Canidae, this succinct energy can uniquely evolve and often reincarnate or re-attach in vaster planes than the carnal dimension.

He'd seen things peering in through the doorway during the night, and they mixed with the smoke that clung to the windows like in a sauna. He'd seen a hand holding a bowl of gifts and food. Some bare feet strung with gold beaded anklets. Some wide eyes with long lashes, seductive and penetrating, dark, like an elephant's eyes. He'd seen a face in the middle of the living room, and it belonged to a body that existed only in his head. It was dressed in white, draped in flowing cloth like a tunic. The fifteen-year-old liked its leanness, its long hands, its dark skin. It blinded him. A man in a three-piece suit had instructed him to look into the person's eyes, to recognize him. The fifteen-year-old entered into them as if into a galaxy, seeing everything and nothing. Now, in the morning, the touch of his mother's hand seemed to materialize it all. She was happy he'd decided to return to the temple.

The mosaic will be a prayer. It will give us a way to access the multiple dimensions of our human avatar.

The temple yard thronged with taffeta skirts and gray suits. The teenagers were in the middle of a circle, wearing jeans and T-shirts, sporting backpacks and headphones, excited by their physical proximity. They barely heard the pastor's sermon, although it specifically addressed them.

It is why a dog will bark, or a household cat will move in quick reaction to energies unseen by the human eye.

The fifteen-year-old snickered with his friends and returned the little punches the girls dealt out in an attempt to catch their attention.

So we tell you to keep in mind that the true origin, the eternal source and power of your Divine Intelligence and consciousness has never been rooted in the physical.

The fifteen-year-old thought he'd heard the same thing a thousand times in his mother's amens, in his teachers' words, and on TV, so he immediately lost interest. He added his voice to the others' laughter, but he was interrupted by a bolt of lightning that forced him to close his eyes. As soon as he tried to open them and figure out where it came from, the bolt neutralized his vision again.

For if the physical brain with the ego personality were unscreened, and thus fully aware of the vast and constant barrage of telepathic communications that do impinge upon it, it would have a most difficult time retaining a sense of identity in linear perception.

He squinted around him, using his hand as a visor. Just before the next reflection hit, he saw a young man in a white shirt near the pastor. He was rotating his wrist to make the sun glance off his watch and straight into the fifteen-year-old's eyes.

You have in current times largely forgotten how much you learned from all of the Beings of the Animal-Kingdom.

They didn't look at each other. The fifteen-year-old turned and watched the glint of light glancing off the summery clothing of his friends, seeking him.

Our design will strive to make a world as it was made when we ourselves were created. To achieve this, we need only use our imaginations.

The fifteen-year-old got to see him up close when they assembled the registration tables for the summer workshops. The pastor had printed several sentences from his sermon in italics as part of the brochure.

Mankind learned survival techniques, and indeed social behavior by not only watching the animals, but also by directly communicating telepathically with them.

The fifteen-year-old felt that he hadn't ever learned to do anything because he didn't have a father. With his mother's eyes fixed on his back, he approached the information table to ask about the arts-and-crafts workshop. He picked up the pencil to write down his name, but it slipped from his fingers. The white-shirted pastor's son was seated there to answer questions, the lightning bolt watch glinting in his eyes. The fifteen-year-old marveled at the lusciousness that rippled through his stomach when they greeted each other with a secret handshake. He wondered where it had gone—the easy soul that had always guided his body until now. The pastor's son wanted to know if he was good with his hands, because making a mosaic required some level of skill. The fifteen-year-old's lip twitched. He took two steps backward after signing his name and lobbed the pencil at the pastor's son with an unfamiliar aggression.

A mosaic will be a body, the materialization of our collective body

Some days, when his mother went out early, he'd stay home on his PlayStation. But that morning he just listened to music and painted the little pieces, following the model given to him by the pastor's son, who studied art at a community institute. Looking out the window, the boy remembered the slashed pants and paint-stained red shirt, the pastor's son murmuring in Creole through the unruly locks that covered his face.

The feline operate vastly in the ethereal or stealth antimatter realm.

When he felt his own hunger and the reek of weed outside, he'd rummage for tobacco in his mother's nightstand and sit on the steps to roll a cigarette. The cool air would come. The smell of damp earth. Shoots burgeoning in the planters out front. Barking dogs. Children fighting over a bicycle, over the sizes of their bodies.

He lit his cigarette and texted Kuan. He shared a photo of his smoke-wreathed face. A strange grazing of the leaves, the violent shudder of the leaves in the planters, made him lift his eyes from the phone. For a moment, he remembered the ethereal presences the pastor had preached about. Maybe, now that he'd returned to the temple, a supernatural being was manifesting itself to him. Such things happened to sensitive people and to prophets, it was said.

The thick two-toned hairs of an animal body appeared among the lush branches of the Chinese evergreen and the ferns. The white and brownish colors were barely distinguishable from the mosses darkening the damp ground. It had found a soft cushion to curl up on. He could see its bulgy head, a smattering of bare patches that showed a tender flesh the same color of certain human skins, like Kuan's. Two dark eyes fixed the boy like pistols. Its ears pricked at the slightest movement. For a few seconds, the animal's and the boy's bodies were perfectly still. The impact of this presence froze his fingers around the cigarette. Then the possum turned its head and rested it on its front paws again. Showing its back, it fell asleep, as if there weren't another creature a hundred times its size a mere foot away. The blood started to flow back into the boy's gangly limbs. He grasped his phone. Before easing it into his pocket and gently rising to his feet, he lifted his arm in a tremulous trance and pressed the shutter button on the screen. His legs could scarcely hold him up. He slipped behind the door. Protected now, he peered out at the animal through the dirty glass.

Back upstairs, he couldn't bring himself to keep drawing. His brush turned the palette to grays and browns. There would be rats in the mosaic, he decided. He'd hang them from their tails, he thought, pacing around the living room like a cage. He was invaded by possible images of a savage rodent. He thought about how to scare it away. Perched on the windowsill, he could still see its body, coiled and lethargic, sleeping in the planter. The sixth or seventh time, he noticed the cigarette butt he'd abandoned on the stairs. When his mother came home, he'd give himself away. Not looking, he sent the photo to Kuan, who responded with a vomiting emoji. The boy steadied the tremble in his hand against the broomstick and went downstairs.

There will be stains. Up here, we will draw a circle that will contain a cicada and other creatures. In each panel, we will observe a detail of an insect painted with a single-bristle brush.

He couldn't take his eyes off the full lips of the pastor's son. He was able to tell Kuan about it once they'd kissed.

These physical formats of the Feline family on the EarthPlane are here to support you, and in their physical matrix are but a portion of the consciousness of their Sirian nature.

The Sirian nature of the pastor's son.

His words triggered something strange between them. A rupture, or maybe a silent understanding. The fifteen-year-old couldn't quite figure it out.

On Saturday night, he told him, the group of mosaic-makers had come together in an act of artistic sleeplessness to start the mural on the western side of the temple. By candlelight, after they'd eaten, the pastor's son gripped a candombe drum between his legs and recited something in a language that the fifteen-year-old could only decipher snatches of. It was about an encounter between a wanderer and an animal on a flowering plain.

The psychic abilities and aspects of cats have long been recognized. They have been desired as partners, allies and protectors by mystics, healers and shamans.

The song began like this: the wandering man hears a growl among the dry leaves and he glimpses what some people call an ilion through the foliage. It's a kind of feline, with a large jaw and bloodied feet. Its teeth study the wandering man. If the encounter between a human and an animal comes to pass, then a third field emerges, a collective one. Thou needest understand, the pastor's son recited to the beat, that this third combination appears by mutual agreement. This third consistency feeds on the encounter, on the fear of the wandering man.

Or something like that, retorted the fifteen-year-old. A lioness's tooth on every chip of tile, he imagined, recalling the voice of the pastor's son. Kuan listened intently to the fifteen-year-old retell it:

The wandering man stumbled along, tripping on his own fear, utterly overwhelmed in the underbrush. His blind, hurried steps led him on steep and arduous paths, over hills and along cliffs. He lost his way in the landscape. Any sound behind made him duck his head and hide. The nocturnal horizon abruptly filled with insects. There were thousands of them, and they scuttled toward the wandering man, who was alone and who was going who knows where or why. Fleeing his captors, perhaps, or his employers, or his family, or something else he didn't want to see. Hordes of animals advanced in his direction, as well as small beings that snarled and raveled at his feet. Rodents and snakes. His footsteps left wet stamps as if he'd walked on water. He fell. Soft flesh beneath his boots. Then came the cattle, whose charge he withstood by pressing himself against a rock, and then the jaws of hungry coyotes. The wandering man watched them with the moon at his back. In the hills. He dug a pit and covered himself with earth so they wouldn't catch his scent. He buried himself as if he were already dead. He woke with the sun and rose because something was hurting his back. The crushed rabbit was damp and warm, all white from nose to tail, entirely caked in mud. Not even its blood was still red.

That's when the drum stopped, said the fifteen-year-old, finishing his story. Silently, he remembered that the voice of the pastor's son had stopped then, too. The candles had melted down. The only clearly visible thing was the white shirt in the middle of the semi-circle of young people sitting close together in the temple yard. Beneath it, he could also make out the muscled body of the pastor's son, agitated by the trance and his own breathing. He told them what they had to do: along with the story of Maîtresse Jill, their ascended teacher, which would be channeled as a sacred message, they would evoke an animal avalanche in the mosaic.

On the right piece, a cat in a white shirt with a drum.

The fifteen-year-old and Kuan kissed one last time and promised each other, fingers entwined, to listen to the same album as they walked back to their homes.

A sheep's long cheekbones.

The streets were calm, the bedroom lights switched off in almost every house he passed. Only a scattering of men shifted among cars and buses.

The cat will often lay on the area and purr.

Tensed bodies flashed beneath the cars. The cats stared out with their crystalline eyes and treaded with silent, unerring steps. They climbed the trees, vaulted roofs and fences, scratched at doors. They slipped along edges and through orifices. The males were clearly distinguishable from the females. The latter slinked through the boy's legs, waiting for his hands to touch them. If he could have, the fifteen-year-old would have taken them home to pet them all night long.

Without his earbuds in, he heard an unsettling silence outside his house. He opened the gate and caught sight of it all at once. It was probably male, judging by the prominence of its jaw. His fur had lost its sheen. His whiteness must have shone in the moonlight once. The cat was bigger than average and any passer-by might have assumed he was asleep. But not the boy. He could tell from where he stood. The cat wasn't curled up, as cats tend to do. His body was deserted of itself. His open eyes looked like empty hollows. Not a trace of light or soul lit up their globes. Maybe someone was working witchcraft so his mom would finally sell the house. The face of the pastor's son returned to him. Animals aren't witchcraft, he would have said.

Without waking his mother, he found her fold-up shopping cart and a shovel and spread a black bag open on top of the cart. He tried to scoop the shovel under the cat's compact body, but the heat had glued its liquids to the pavement. When it finally gave, an uncertain smell invaded the air and a smattering of insects vanished through chinks and fissures in the stone wall. He laid the body onto the cart as best he could. On his way to the park, the white tail dropped straight down and he had to readjust it several times with the shovel. Slowly, he got used to the lifeless presence. He dug a hole, small but deep, in a secluded corner between the trees and the gate of the adjacent school. He had to hide repeatedly from the police lights and a few men staggering around from bench to bench, talking to themselves. He finished late and wept.

Lips that could explain all this.

The skin will be several shades of gray to evoke the motion of walking. From a distance, we'll watch it wind its way through the branches made of green tile shards.

He dreamed of wasps. They appeared in the shower. He saw blood on the tiles, but he couldn't figure out where it came from. His mother woke him. She picked up the bowl with the remnants of incense sticks from his nightstand. Heavy-lidded, he watched her peel the screen from the window and toss out the ash. She walked back to the bed and stroked his face and hair. I got the wasp out of here, she said, as if she'd stepped right into his dream. I like knowing you're safe, she said, smoothing her hands over the bedsheet. The fifteen-year-old sat up with a start. There's no temple today and it's hot out. Why don't you go off to the beach. Don't your friends go to the beach? He accepted the kisses she planted on the top of his head and he rubbed his eyes. He didn't want to go to the beach. He had to see the pastor's son. His mother looked at him, puzzled. A smile spread across her face, flooding it completely. There was no cause for her joy but divine intervention. Don't forget the bug spray. The mosquitos are out of control today.

When this partnership occurs these beings are able to telepathically receive thought images sent by their caretaker.

The breakfast table was set. It was a blessing that there was anything more than cheap cereal. There was a certain happiness, the boy noted, in pleasing his mother, and in how he found that happiness in the lips of the pastor's son. A wasp paused on his toast. He looked at it intently and followed it with his eyes all the way to the hole in the screen. He felt a prick.

The long mane of the pastor's son showing him the way.

The blow to his arm spilled his blood and left the liquid remains of the mosquito's body smeared across his ring finger.

To install a mosaic on cement, we will need a trowel or spatula, a sponge or rag, a hammer, a bolt cutter, some plaster, and some adhesive or white cement.

They're bigger than average. It was the voice of the pastor's son behind him. The fifteen-year-old had reached the building before the others. They stood with their faces near the gate for a long time, studying the half-finished mosaic: the orange of some wings, the green of the foliage, the black of the rats just grazing the ground, the several grays of the feline that the fifteen-year-old was shading in. They were so close that the fifteen-year-old could smell the soap, deodorant, and sweat on the body of the pastor's son. The fifteen-year-old's eyes took in the body next to his. Their eyes met. He'd never noticed it before: a certain motion in the eyes of the pastor's son that made them two-toned, deeper, more disconcerting.

There is a choice to accept the human on the part of the Felidae (or not). This third meld occurs by mutual agreement.

The pastor's son's whistles were recognized indoors. The pastor emerged in suit pants and sandals, shirtless, scattering a cloud of mosquitoes.

Golden and silvery fish leaping as if rupturing clouds in the sea, soothing an infestation.

Kuan and the fifteen-year-old decided to walk along the edge, towels over their shoulders. Kuan guided him across a beach where people were spaced farther apart, swam naked, and smoked marijuana. Their hands touched in the warm water that lulled them like a cradle. Hungry, the fifteen-year-old felt the salt on Kuan's lips. They made their way along the back path. The dry branches shadowed Kuan's face. They undressed. They kissed each other's entire bodies. They pleasured each other with their mouths. Seeing all of Kuan was new to the fifteen-year-old. Feeling everything was new. He saw the long cheekbones of a sheep in Kuan's features, the narrow eyes of a wolf cub, the brightness of a parrot, the muscled hooves of a fawn, and the mane of the pastor's son.

His hat collecting his dreadlocks to make it easier.

The wet between his legs slicked together with the damp of the sea. They stretched out to smoke a joint, rinsed out their trunks, and went back to the beach. They walked, picking their way among the fishing lines, until they reached the structures that hadn't been demolished by the hurricane. Three or four raised huts stood at the edge. Latino families inhabited the first and most ravaged of the lot. In the others, men and women sat in chairs, their skin reddened by the sun. The kids walked quickly, feeling eyes on them that identified their foreign accents and warm complexions. The beach opened out and they could see the end of the island in the distance. They latched onto the thought that they were witnessing the vast Atlantic. Seaweed tangled around their toes. They crossed the kingdom of seagulls poised on their eggs, the mosquitoes swirling among them, a certain air of rot. They glimpsed a group of people. They were pulling cans out of a cooler and wearing the newest clothes they'd ever seen. If the kids kept walking, it was because they felt invincible together. They talked. They smoked. They kissed and held hands.

They are brilliant divinely intelligent Crystalline-Light Beings, nonphysical from your perspective. They are masters of incorporating spirit into physicality and assisted in the original engineering of full strand DNA for mankind.

Before they came to the first beach chairs with a poster that said private property no trespassing, they saw the corpse of a turtle. It was five feet long, its shell was broken, and it was decaying and infested with larvae inside. A vulture watched them defiantly from close by. The stench was overpowering. It was almost impossible to believe that eight reddish-blond men were silently enjoying the ocean just a few yards away. A little farther off, a woman was tending to some children. She spoke to them in Spanish as she covered her nose with a handkerchief. They did the same. Uneasy, they decided to retrace.

We will stick the pieces together with a little plaster, which we will make out of white cement and apply with a spatula.

He was no longer sure whether it was the insect bites or the toxic repellent that had irritated his skin. He pulled his T-shirt back on. The air was so humid that the cloth instantly clung to his long torso. He paused for a moment under the trees in front of my house, where I was writing, and stretched his arms. The fifteen-year-old had grown taller lately. He moved without the fragility of a new thing.

We listened to the calm of the slow summer morning, which was quickly interrupted by a dog howling in a nearby house. We went still. They were howls of pain. Some new neighbors stopped to deliberate over whether they should ring the bell and call the police as the dog's anguish grew louder and shriller.

He is equally conscious of being fully manifested simultaneously in other dimensional planes. Quite often they interact within the other realms, while present physically in this one.

The howls suddenly stopped. After a few minutes, the new neighbors turned and walked away. But the fifteen-year-old didn't, and neither did I, observing the scene from my front steps. After a few moments, a woman emerged from the house where the howls had been. She opened the gate and started her car. Bellowing, the fifteen-year-old forced her into the vehicle. She screeched away without shutting the gate. Murderer, he screamed, then sat down on the sidewalk with tears in his eyes and held his head in his hands.

There was another dog a few doors down. In the summer, his ivory arctic fur was a torment. He had one green eye and the other was a blue so pale it was nearly white. A gentler animal had never walked the earth. It was as if all his wildness had been beaten out of him. After noon, the owners of the house would leave the dog tied to the gate on a short leash in the blazing sun. He struggled with all his might to fend off the rats that crept out of the garbage heap.

The fifteen-year-old couldn't take his eyes off the dog. He opened the gate, called him by name, and stroked his head. Docile, the dog let the boy wet his head with water. He didn't make a sound when the fifteen-year-old knelt before it. When the father of the house peered out at the scene through the grates of the air conditioner, the boy raised his fist. A few days later, the dog was gone.

Once the pieces are in place, wet a cloth with water only—no thinner—and wipe them to remove any remnants of cement plaster.

The fifteen-year-old dodged the tourists as they surged out of the elevator. Before he stepped in, he photographed the glass tube that would take him up the 136 stories of the tower.

The Beings that we term animals operate in great and greater intelligence, albeit in a thought-pattern matrix uniquely formatted to the natural aspect of the Earth-Plane.

Inside, he found the pastor's son all by himself, his arms stretched out along the elevator's metal railing as he leaned back against it. You're late, he said. Everyone else already left.

The fifteen-year-old's body instantly drained of all the strength he'd felt surging through him as he and his earbuds made their way upstream, following the human current through Midtown. He lowered his eyes to his legs so they wouldn't turn to wool. But you're still here, he said by way of greeting, standing in the center of the elevator. Where is it? he asked. The pastor's son replied with a gesture, signaling through the glass, pressing the highest number on the elevator interface. The metal doors shut only halfway, and the elevator suddenly filled with tourists, all wearing T-shirts of the same color and carrying backpacks and cameras. Their steps were short as they distributed themselves, looking down at the floor and nudging the fifteen-year-old subtly toward his companion. The final push landed him mere millimeters from the pastor's son, from his white shirt, his long hair, his delicious sweat-smell. The pastor's son didn't take his arms from the railing, and so their arms grazed each other with a rhythmic softness.

The elevator started upward, leaving the skyscraper's glass lobby behind, rising above the picture windows, the awnings of the stores across the street, the people shopping in department stores. The fifteen-year-old turned to watch as they abandoned the roofs of the other buildings down below, the chimneys, the occasional balcony, and discovered the roughshod tin sheets that mark the tops of buildings in New York. He felt his stomach come to life with a vertigo that morphed into something else, spurred by the nearby breath of the pastor's son and the brush of his arm when he grabbed the railing to steady his balance.

One of the tourists let out a phobic yelp and jostled his way forward, demanding to be let out. He sweated and clutched his temples. As soon as the elevator stopped, the tourists threw themselves at the exit, leaving such a piercing silence in their wake that the fifteen-year-old wondered whether the pastor's son could hear his heartbeat. Here we go again, said the pastor's son. The elevator kept rising and the boys, hands clutching the rail, watched the city plummet away from them as their bodies turned into clammy cathodes. On the 78th floor, they saw flocks of birds streak past with pointy wings and orange breasts. The fifteen-year-old's imagination flew off with them for a moment.

He saw the beginning. On the façade of the skyscraper in front of them, peeking through smaller buildings, the yellow of the mosaic appeared, framed in blue. That's how I learned to make them a few years ago, said the pastor's son. Like you right now. This is all that's left of that summer. The pastor's son pressed the stop button as he said this. He said, not every emergency is a call for help.

The mosaic glimmered. In the middle were the bare feet adorned with gold beads. Its many hands were laden with gifts and food, its head wreathed in gold like a holy corolla. Its trunk wound around its body and the boy immediately recognized its deep, seductive eyes, like an amethyst of his hallucinations. Around the central form, various drawings of birds formed celestial figures that were cats, dogs, humans, skunks, and anteaters. Insects were beginning to accumulate beyond the window and the fifteen-year-old looked down at the 136 floors beneath him and his legs dissolved. But his body didn't collapse. The fingers of the pastor's son had entwined at the nape of his neck. Heart in hand, the fifteen-year-old saw a panther's face bring its lips to his, streaking his limbs with a tingle that didn't feel like it belonged to him. His mosquito legs became one with the arachnid threads of the pastor's son. Outside, the sun had faded and clouds of bumblebees hovered zealously around the birds that unspooled their spiritual choreographies in the last rays of sunlight. The fifteen-year-old was cornered. On top of him, the body of the pastor's son held him captive, his horse-legs beating over the dunes, his fish-mouth waiting to receive, and the sky was water and he heard himself make the sound of a sheep whose throat is slit before the slaughter.

When we're done, we will look at the mosaic together and behold what we once were.

They'd gotten dressed quickly when the elevator shifted back into motion. The city was dark by then. Between the buildings, though, he could still make out the last glimmer of sun flashing on the other, earlier mosaic that the pastor's son had installed with another temple group. There were the trunk and the feet, the cloth golden as a crown.

What was different from what he'd experienced on the beach with Kuan? he wondered, sidestepping passers-by on his way to the subway. And he also wondered whether what he felt for the pastor's son, a sensation he'd collected and harbored for nearly four months now, would vanish as swiftly as what he'd felt for Kuan. In the days before the start of the new school year, he'd stopped feeling the need to see Kuan, and his legs didn't weaken when they stood together to look at the finished mosaic.

On the first day of school, the fifteen-year-old didn't eat the cereal his mother had set out for him, and he left early on his bike to visit the mosaic. The temple yard was still cluttered with remnants of the goodbye party the pastor had thrown for his son when he went away to college. Kuan was gone, too, having left for Wisconsin, family and all. In the fog, the colors of the mosaic on the western wall gleamed onto the street. He saw the figure of the cat again, his own ilion, which looked like it was made of thousands of other beings unfolded into branches and mosquitos. The bird section plummeted toward the rats that emerged from the bottom of the frame and seemed to set their claws on the edge of the street. Along one side, a tree rose up that sheltered the sleeping possum, a rabbit, and some squirrels. In the middle of the scene, near his feline, came whole flocks of southern animals: the surges of swine, the clatters of colts, the mysteries of mares. The shoals flashed across the frame, painting a sky that wouldn't have existed without the sunflower of their skins. And in the middle of it all, its naked feet with beads around their ankles, its deep, seductive eyes, its trunk furled around its body. All that would be left of that summer was the mosaic. Nothing more. And he decided he'd never go back to the temple again.

The Object

I slept through the entire hour-long subway ride from my place in Crown Heights to the neighborhood in upper Manhattan that was supposed to be called something else now. The change didn't hurt anything, says the man in the seat across from mine, smiling immensely. Now we all get to be here. The doors snap shut. I realize I've left my book on the seat, the one by José Emilio Recabarren I'd checked out of the library. Accepting the loss, I make my way toward the object.

The small door amid all the restored buildings makes me nervous, especially when I walk into the bookstore, where the few customers turn to glance at me sidelong. It occurs to me that I have no interest in these objects, nor they in me. Only a couple catch my eye. Small presses, tasteful editions, the names of the translators putting the other, larger names in perspective.

I pick up an object I think Carlos would find interesting and examine it carefully. Meanwhile, in a corner, a man with the beard of a retired scientist and a too-red nose addresses a young man who's just opened his eyes and tells him how space can be folded. The young man's mouth looks hungry for the first taste of an object whose tips and edges he tries to decipher. The old man moves closer to show him how it's done. The young man lets his teeth show and finds my eyes, making room for me to answer him somehow.

The books are piled up on the sides of the stairs, the authors' names overlaid like raw material. With my gaze alone, I select the ones I'd like to take with me but know I'll never buy, counting, given the state I'm in, the coins in my pockets. As I reach the second floor of the bookstore, I nearly stumble. I leave my footprint on the open pages of a DeLillo book. There's a vast open space with maybe seven rows of seats blocking the way. The organizers are expecting an enormous crowd. But only two seats are taken. I glance at the clock: it's almost time for the launch of Gordon Lish's latest short story collection to begin.

The books are piled up on the shelves and I notice that the store sells textbooks to Columbia students. Several of them vanish into the aisles, arms laden. A well-dressed man sits on the stairs to read a book about Fanon, but he shuts it and opens a different one, trying to hide the title. Standing at the end of the aisle, I see an old armchair positioned in the middle of the makeshift stage, clearly chosen to grant the venue a literary air. The armchair is the object, I hear one of the macabre old men say as they chatter edgily and tilt their heads toward the back of the space.

I sit in the third row, behind some women who quickly move closer to the stage when the man in the armchair asks them to. Farther back, the seats are still empty. The man with white hair, vampiric skin, and a raspy voice requests once again that we advance toward the object. I am the object, he says. The chairs in front of me have been bottlenecked by the women's movements, so I stay where I am. The object takes offense at this and uses it as an incentive to expound on the meaning of art and how apprentice writers ought to approach the object. Gordon Lish presents a series of anecdotes to illustrate his point: when he worked at *Esquire*, he covered a convention held by Exxon to whitewash their image. Several Nobel Prize-winners were invited to speak. Like any good reporter, he refers to everyone he can remember by name. Like any good tyrant, he orders the audience to repeat them. All men. All gringos. I notice that all of the people occupying a miniscule fraction of the available seats are employed either by the bookstore or by the press, except for me. Lish continues to elucidate his object theory using several of his own disciples: those who approached the object versus those who followed other paths in life. He disdains the second group. He praises one whose name appears in the credits of TV shows no one has seen, another who's been nominated for an award, and a woman whose name he can't remember. He also evokes various disciples he has edited himself. He makes a few mathematical calculations and divides humanity into people who approach the object and people who approach money. For some reason, he says, he got both.

I consider leaving. Then Lish mentions DeLillo, one name in a long list of authors, and I'm intrigued by the coincidence.

All are friends of his, he explains. He prattles on about his power over dead writers. I finally decide to take a photo of the object. But he's offended by the black square I hold in front of my face and he curses me. The members of the audience are uncomfortable, but he won't cede the floor, and he eventually suggests that they ask him questions. No one dares to speak. One woman looks down at the glass of wine she's been holding for the past thirty or forty minutes. She doesn't know if she should or can raise the glass to her lips, her body frozen in an endless yes. The object has taken over the audience. Suddenly, we all shift into impatience, we all want the launch to be over. We all feel a little bit of contempt, a little bit of pity for the object.

He never leaves his house, he says then. He's walked the two blocks here as an exception. He usually just looks out his window uncomprehendingly as the world changes down below. All that motion, all those people, all those colors, he rasps. Coughing a time or two, he decides to stop talking. No one buys his book.

All of us are outside the bookstore. Inside is a city that no longer exists. Outside, we can breathe. Inside is anxiety, the fear of a tyrannical white man who watches with horror and rage as the world transforms around him, as if it were the code to some indecipherable science. Outside, space has twisted into folds, a spiral where our very breathing grants it those multiple universes. The city fades away with every block: the city of shortage, poverty, excess, the centripetal force of fantasy, the void where bombs and fish rain down.

I take the bus home instead of the subway so I can feel the air and the light. Two hours to my apartment in Crown Heights. I hold a rare English-language translation of *The Night of Tlatelolco*, photocopied and unbound. As the bus moves east and down below the island of Manhattan, leaving it behind, the city shows its tips, reveals its edges, the colors change, it teems with objects that puncture cameras. The movie theaters fill with local audiences speaking languages that smudge and mix together, identities grow liquid and numerous. The streets throng and people follow other logics to understand that the New York we're all leaving behind is not the object anymore.

Invocation

For J and C

The walls in the first-floor room, where I've been led by the woman down a long hallway, are sound-proofed with egg cartons, and the single double-paned window looks out onto a large garden with a little table in the sun. Before the writer stands and holds out her cold, gnarled hand—her right is stained with dark greenish ink—I hear how silently she writes. The only noise is a faint, mantric sound emerging from a cheap little speaker on a corner of the desk. The first thing she does, the woman who's led me there, is to open the window, letting the wind and the rustle of new leaves seep in. The two women who live in the house exchange mistrustful glances. The writer addresses me in a heavy

You ask the questions. I'll limit myself to answering them. You must know that excessive attention exacerbates my asthma. My condition demands specific measures of besiegement, affection, and endearment, if they're to vanish from our shared horizon.

You ask about my ear. Imagine, if you will, that you were so lucky as to consult a specialist who could selectively erase your memories. I don't know what you'd ask of him, but I'd certainly request that he erase as many sound-memories as possible, so that I could experience hearing them for the first time. Can you imagine what it would be like to encounter a piece of music, or a performance on an instrument accent, inviting me to sit in a small armchair beside the window, facing a table set with two cups of tea. She rejects the other woman's every offer of a drink, although, once we're alone, she pours herself a cup of what I myself have been served. I have to give her a couple pats on the back after her first sip. She gestures almost violently for me to stop.

I turn on the voice recorder and repeat my endlessly rehearsed introduction about why I'm conducting this interview, careful never to mention our past association. She asks me to remind her where it's going to be published and she raises an eyebrow at my answer. I carry on for a bit, trying to decipher whether she's understood or simply stopped listening altogether. And so I interrupt myself to ask her why she's soundproofed the walls. I let her speak, shifting my pencil

as glorious as a piano, or the voice of someone you love as if it had never before existed, but without forgetting everything else that has made you what you are? In the absence of such a thing, I have this and my fantasies to drive it all away—what I find pleasant and what I don't. You'll understand when you've gone. The idea is to inhabit the everlasting.

You ask why I bother writing about a subject as common as love after my successive works on death, illness, and ghosts. I felt that I was running out of time, and that my writing invoked the actions I'd find myself engaged in soon after. Meanwhile, outside, were all the indications of true disaster. The streets teemed with death and the work was increasingly arduous. I endured it with greater and greater hunger. A student in Germany who read my texts attentively was the from one hand to the other. This way I can look at her calmly and for a long time. I'm struck by her masculine hands, their short nails, dry skin, no rings. She hasn't aged much. It's so strange that she doesn't remember me. I've heard her vision has started to fail. She couldn't take her eyes off me when we met. The tremors that crept through our bones and lower bellies whenever we ran into each other—it was a joy, and a kind of curse, this constant feeling-outside-of-ourselves in the other's presence. We'd avoid each other, but everyone else could tell what was going on.

Her nearness was like an illness in me.

I remember reading *The Sorrows of Young Werther* as a teenager, my face tight with derision. As if killing yourself over a heartbreak

the one who made me see it. And so I set out to write about things that endure over time. I wanted to integrate the freedom I'd experienced with my partners and lovers into my tormented spirit. I wanted to create an other, beyond me.

You ask about the image of the nursing child that appears in the novel. No, I'm not interested in filial relationships; I'm interested in the prototype of all romantic relationships, in the image that represents the search for the beloved object. The topic of physical nutrition also comprises the possibility of feeding one's spirit, experienced in love and in sexual satisfaction. Representing love in this way thus manifests desire in close affiliation with a culture of care that doesn't necessarily inhabit the genital areas. Contained in this image, then, which we find in the paintings of Christian and proto-Christian were something alien, a thing of the past. More than a decade after shedding my immaturity, my body unexpectedly experienced childish feelings—and for someone I never would have admired beyond a stirring of murderous resentment.

In the first months I knew you, I felt something like the pain Werther felt for Charlotte: it made me scorn and desire you at the same time. My vulnerability intensified because I was broke, really trapped in a state of total precariousness despite the books I'd published and the occasional award I'd won for my political writing. I thought that you, an immigrant like myself, would understand what it meant to take on that kind of job, so far removed from my area of expertise. But you harbored unresolved oedipal feelings that eventually surfaced between us. They appeared like an egg between my thighs,

culture, is the seed of a feminine love that my work seeks to explore.

You ask about my love life. My answer is that this has nothing to do with what I write. The novel you hold in your hands is an invocation.

I'd like to inform you that we're straying from our subject, because my answer is simply a copy of the mental image of the perfect answer, never more than an effect. Your questions remind me of my past: the images of absent bodies that spread from the page to the screen, from the screen to the scene, and then to a mock-up in which the scene could eventually be filmed with dolls. What could possibly express love better than a copy? All the images that have seeped into us, affixed themselves to our bodies. All the images we recognize in our gestures. Perhaps love is simply the imitation blossomed forth from my navel, sprouted like the head of a ram on the other's neck. Your childlike sadism, your utter need to see your desires fulfilled, materialized with me, an insect on my tail, an ache in my back. There were things I was unwilling to do, particularly after I'd finished the philosophy book that would bring me such good fortune a few years later. But you needed something else—entertainment, perhaps. What else could you want in that idyllic, painless present you bore like a burden? You saw me as a lost mother of sorts, someone you could use to enact all your sadistic impulses. The feeling—hidden deep inside you, though it asserted itself intensely—that women, and the woman who inhabited you, were contemptible. In me, you could embody all your hatred of yourself.

Once, I remember, when I'd come

of words, writings, works for the stage. What I ask myself is how to experience love after all those descriptions that tell us how to love. And I'm obsessed with how, in spite of it all, the whole melodrama that's performed in gazes and violent gestures is experienced as something utterly unique.

You ask about the paradox contained in the love between women, a secret, uncharted territory manifested in the brush of a hand, a strangeness barely populated by words.

You ask about the girl's evolution into womanhood in the novel. I can't respond with anything other than what I already wrote: "The sun rose out of a hollow in the Andes Mountains, like a woman's face with her gold beads tumbling down the slopes, filling the dryland bushes with a yellow clamor.

to the theater, you asked me to watch the rehearsal of a scene I wasn't in. The actors were personifying a drama of submission you'd decided to light obliquely with a bluish glow that granted the scene a kind of crushing coldness. It ended in total silence, and when the actors were done, you gave me a tender smile, handing me your jacket with a series of incoherent instructions, as if you were rehearsing a scene with me, too. I remember that I walked out of the rehearsal room, and before I shut the door behind me, I tossed the jacket into a box that was designated for discarded wardrobe items. A little later, sitting in front of the mirror to review my lines, I saw you reappear with the jacket hung over your shoulders, not saying a word.

Looking at the stage from up above, I see the ground shift like water, see characters whose fluidity

By this time of day, the mosquitos were sipping their way along the row of walls, lashed away by striped lancets. Resounding, too, was the buzz and the movements of the man in his little cart rattling up dust from the cold dirt road. He peered through the bushes and saw the legs of a naked girl stretched out on a bed of poppies. He made sure that she hadn't been dismembered and said to himself there she is. The mosquitos suddenly retreated and the girl dreamed that a river of stones and insects flowed out from between her legs. Writhe, flushed and embodied. The little girl's eyes closed every time she tried to open them. As the man in the cart approached her, he saw that she was dreaming of him. He mounted his horse. The sun was staring straight ahead by now, and only a trail of dust was left high up in the mountains. The girl had had sensual dreams all night long and addresses the two of us, reflects us. The lights go out, and as the actors recover their breath, I see your face, transforming into a body that doesn't seem like mine. Liquid trickles out from between those legs.

Over the next few days, during rehearsal, you reappear wherever you aren't, impeding my diction. Sometimes you look me in the eye. Sometimes your stark profile tilts toward me. Other days, when we run into each other in the halls, I see a light emanating from your chest, my vision blurs, and I experience your footsteps as a blow to my stomach that forces me onto my knees before you. Feeling the tips of my breasts go firm, my voice falters.

In rehearsals, I no longer understand what the actors are saying or where the banal storyline is

wasn't sure what kind of hard body was protruding from the end of her buttocks, her feet now downy with lanugo. She went home to her parents' house, slipping in through the window, and stood at the foot of their bed. Look a cat, they said. And they decided to keep it, maybe recognizing a sort of sadness in her eyes."

You ask about the girl when she's almost a teenager. I can't respond without citing what I've already written: "The dew fell as if in small flames. Through the window, she could see her mother feeling the iris buds that had risen up from among the varicose pistils with her fingertips. The mother, like the dawn, seized one whose leaves were scattered across the ground, drawing Ss over the meadows. The cat's tail instinctively swirled and shuddered, prompting a loud screech. The inhabitants of the headed: a plot you've put together by dint of massive budgets and luxurious wardrobes brimming with costumes that must cost as much as the foreign actress's salary. Images pass before my eyes as on a screen, or like the act of hypnosis. Any nearby body could feel the force of it.

The first dream came to me in the form of a vampire, reading at a table in a library. My hands held some loose papers and I was annotating them. In the dream, I couldn't manage to stay awake. Unfolded in this way, I could see, from the other end of the room, my lashes fluttering shut with fatigue, my head dropping backward toward the back of the chair, a set of teeth piercing my neck. When I woke up, two old men with books in their hands were staring at me, each in his respective corridor.

mountainside peered out their windows at her.

The room with the cat in it filled with the smell of tobacco and the windowpane misted up. She felt the father's eyes dense at the base of her back, where golden curls tumbled down. Through them, she felt the semi-smile of the face framed by thick hair, white and tangled. The father caressed her lower back and said those irises are like your curves, I won't let you leave the house with them. But she escaped. She leapt into her mother's arms, the woman too bathed in the yellow dust of her fingers. Clutched in those arms, the cat began to dream of the Virgin Mary, one breast exposed, like in the painting on the wall of the church where she'd go to wait out the afternoon heat. Tiny toothless mouths scratched at the Virgin's smooth skin like little claws, simultaneously stroking her with their white shelter. The

The second dream occurred at the very midpoint between wakefulness and sleep. With my eyes closed, I'd see your profile appear against a dark, wild landscape, your red locks tumbling down your slender neck and the stiff cloth of your white shirt that marked the contours of your body. Your face would suddenly turn to meet mine, staring deep into me. The background would disappear, and with the light that shone forth from your chest, you caught my gaze like a rabbit in the woods at night. Your expression, a perverse fawn, was the light bulb. The sets were varied: a hotel room, a location inspired by countless films. An elevator, like the one you described in your novel. Your house, which I recognized from descriptions alone. The street or any other space with lighting that resembled the kind you'd sketched out in the stairway scene we were rehearsing

milk-nursers would molt. Some of them. Others wouldn't be able to, forced instead to spend their lives in a coat of lanugo. They wanted to nurse so they could stand naked before the eyes, the light bulbs. When she woke, she felt the father's tobacco-smell pacing around behind the rosebushes. The hens were trailing him, and the chicks she longed to chew into bloodlessness, their feathers lined up in a little row. From the window, looking dawnward, she saw the mother with yellowed fingers. The blight scattered onto the grass, into the dust-breeze. The mother brought an iris to her lips and ate it. Then another, until she'd finished every last one. The yellow sores on the mother's face, the falling beads, watering down her neck—she saw it all. Buds blossomed from the cat's striped tail."

You ask about that teenage girl who

at the time. You'd approach me open-palmed and I'd clasp your neck before our bodies touched. You wouldn't stop and my hands would grip harder and harder. With your veins about to rupture, you'd softly place a hand on my cheek, forcing yourself to look at me with those dead-animal eyes. Your lips would draw closer, slowly, and you'd back me up against the wall, and you'd slip anything into me, your fingers, your tongue, a genital prosthesis, as my legs rose up and my hands scraped at the wall behind me. There would be no conversation afterward, and I'd exit stage left.

The third dream was made of images that would overtake me while, sitting at your desk, I reviewed rehearsal schedules and budgets that blistered my fingers with resentment. I'd dream you were ill, on the verge of death, or dead by becomes a woman. As you can see, the transformation was ultimately incomplete, because she's hung with tails, she has a hairy dorsal, a set of claws she uses to scratch the backs of the village men. I'll answer your question with another passage from a book I didn't write: "Her age was exactly what attracted the monsters." I took, from this invocation, the image of a teenager and a long branch she uses to write her name and age in the sand, as if titling an identification file: "Under the grape arbor one summer evening, drowsing against her mother's belly, she felt the earthquake, a kick that shot out directly from inside her mother. She was overcome with fear. She sprouted claws that dug into the mother's naked skin. The pregnant woman's shouts shook their way into the cat's heart, where the tremble lived from then on. The mother flung her aside with a slap and the next my own hand, at the same time as I remained your only salvation, both emotional and physical. I'd dream of you with sores on your arms, indifferent to heat and cold, requiring my every attention. And I'd respond by spitting in your face. Sometimes you'd make requests of me and I'd threaten to hit you until you bled. I'd urinate onto that radiant chest with which you'd introduced yourself to me, and if you were lucky, I'd insert a prosthesis into your anus like a punishment.

You decided to leave for a while to visit your family—and, I suspected, to visit one of your lovers in Paris. My feet didn't know where to rest during your absence. When I'd try to focus on them, the ground would go transparent and I could see the five floors below me, could imagine plummeting down into the abyss, the flocks of mourning doves rising up without

day a hairless child emerged from her belly. The mother's hands now had eyes for nothing but him. The cat roamed on all fours like a *colo-colo*, tail between her legs, feeling an earthquake in her pulse. She struggled to breathe. Her legs weakened and she couldn't vault the walls as easily as before. She fell into a ditch and barely managed to limp her way back into her older brother's room. She settled into a corner of the bed and regarded the rhythm in his chest, those elongated, female features, evoking the mother. She curled up onto his pillow. She coiled around his head as she caught a faint scent of tobacco and freshly cut flowers amid the milk-smell that invaded the bedroom and the sheets. She never left him after that. She molted under his caresses and sometimes forgot all about her tail, which seemed to hide among the folds of her skirts. She now wore them me. I'd barely manage to make out those hands I'd never touched from among their wings, hands that now looked entirely ordinary. When I became myself again, I found messages unanswered. The coldness of your replies pierced me like a knife, my hands bound to your blade. My chest broke out in rashes that resembled the outline of your fingers pressed into me. My texts grew lax, my thinking vague. My notebooks filled with errors: they were incoherent sketches if I didn't add any of your name's secret letters and the rhythms I used to interpret the days when we recognized each other.

During the month you were gone, I put away my pencil for good. I couldn't sleep at night and food felt like an excess unless I forced it down with a glass of wine or hard liquor. All the cigarettes made me cough. The gauntness of my with pompoms, hoop earrings, and organdy. The brother, impeccably behaved, led her on his arm through the pine and cedar door to the annual party. The cloth of the dress, pulled tight with thread and percale, lent a certain sensuality to the music sounding from the speakers. They made their way over to a woman. This is my girlfriend, the brother said. The sister's little glove split open when she extended her hand to the woman, who was maybe thirty-five years old, slender, with symmetrical features, short hair and exquisite manners. When she touched the woman, her torn gloves took on a scent of tobacco and iris, with an acidity she immediately recognized as milk. The woman's arms were uncovered. Visible, too, were the long golden curls that tumbled down her back. Her heart wasn't in her chest anymore. It was earthquaking in the pit of her stomach, in cheekbones, legs, and hips became a source of concern to some. But to others, my livid lips, the dark, low circles ringing my weepy eyes, my stammering throat, the cowed hunch of my back, my hips warped as if by a sprain—they were a magnet now.

I didn't go home for a month. I'd leave the bedrooms of my occasional lovers in their husbands' pants, socks, and boxers. I'd forget my bras under their pillows. In the evenings, I'd touch young women's faces with the same gestures I wanted you to use in touching mine. I'd undress them as I wanted you to undress me. I rehearsed without my prior passion, whiling away the hours in books, rediscovering the mark my pencil could make. I'd go to opening nights with colleagues to whom I'd profess and be professed undying love. I found solace in one. His straight hair,

her legs, in the liquid that trickled from the triangle between the cat's legs and tail."

You ask about the perspective shifts in the novel. I wanted to explore a change in voice toward a place without boundaries between bodies. I'll answer with another excerpt narrated by the thirty-five-year-old girlfriend: "She had seen me in one of the concerts she attended with her brother a few months before we met. We realized this one day, later, when I was already her brother's girlfriend. Looking at her in her bathing suit, I saw that she didn't have a tail anymore, just a protuberance at the front of her legs. With her flat chest, she'd suddenly taken on her brother's figure, but she was graced with a beauty that shone from her like lunar light. The first time we saw each other after her transformation, my eyes deceived me again his dark, deep eyes called out for my care. His drastic thinness, his flat chest, his voice like a purring in my ears. I kissed a man for the first time while dressed as a man. That night, we called each other by all sorts of names as our lips met softly and our clothes jumbled together in embraces that dropped to the ground. We closed our eyes. I was met with the sight of your face in profile, stark like his face, your long, slightly clumsy fingers in his fingers. The desire that manifested in him was your desire. After that night when I spoke your name for the first time, I went home and took off the clothes that didn't belong to me. I pulled on my skirt and my slender, feminine shoes, the bras that exaggerated my cleavage.

You turned around and the first thing you noticed was the fullness of my breasts, my semi-sheer stockings, the shoes that made me

and I struggled to focus on her. It was like staring into a sun. She stood beside me, waiting for me to put down the book I held in my hands. She told me about other writers I hadn't read, emphasizing her superiority despite our difference in age. We spoke for over two hours that day, and though I had serious apprehensions about hiring her, given her youth and her paltry qualifications, the desire that swelled between us obliged me to do so. Without understanding how, her body lodged itself in me during the month we didn't speak. Her smooth voice on the phone was a purring in my ears. That day, I offered my home to her for the first time, saying that there was enough space for her and her cats while she looked for an apartment that would allow her to live near mine. She refused. The second time she came to see me, I was struck by her bare arms, slim and browned by the stumble down the halls. You'd close your legs. When I'd approach you, you'd hide behind the walls. You'd avoid speaking to me altogether so that I wouldn't notice your discomfort. The day I returned from my travels, I told you I'd missed you. I couldn't see your backlit face. You came closer and I could see that your chest was now flat and you had a package of meat between your legs. Your unshaven face, the masculine dryness of your skin. I felt a bit repulsed when you looked me up and down from that body of yours. I repeated the sentence, addressing you with the male pronoun. I was suddenly shot through with a sense of tenderness toward you, like what one might feel for a child.

Now that I was a woman and you were a man, we could comfortably inhabit the stereotype. I could say, then, that our relationship

sun. I could still sense the summer-scent on her skin. We sat so close to each other that our long back-length curls jumbled together."

You ask why I write about melodrama if what I depict in my work is mere crisis. In recent years and their intensifying wars, various battles have been fought on the field of love, mainly over how to forge an adequate form of collectivity. Family can no longer serve as the only foundation for the collective, as we have been led to believe it must. Nor can working relationships, that retrograde hierarchy in which women have always been treated with suspicion. Nothing that can be taken for Greek tragedy, for a myth about the genealogical proximity of everyone who resembles each other in their bodies and features, in their customs and speech. It is, if we consider it with the depth it deserves, a unfolded amid the conventions of a melodrama. It was, as they say, love at first sight, but complications quickly ensued: I was an avowed feminist and you were a happily married member of the bourgeoisie who was embarking on the necessary paperwork to adopt a child with your fourth wife, a well-regarded doctor I met in the emergency room when I fell down the stairs at the theater. As I'd maintained lesbian proclivities in spite of my femme presentation and she was festering with desire for the baby that would come from the same third-world country as I, we forged a bond triangulated by the man you now were. Over subsequent visits to her office, that maternal affection evolved into a confusing love. With you, by contrast, I became a submissive woman, the transformation exacerbated by the cast on my leg, my improbably high heels, the

reductive way to define love's existing potentiality as a social connection. The text in which Alexandra Kollontai addresses young workers, who long to see love as part of a proletarian republic, is rooted in the ideal according to which all intimate acts are also social, and which are likewise at the service of a collective good. Kollontai puts it very innocently—pedagogically, I'd say—so that the youths would integrate their desire for other bodies into the proletarian project. By contrast, in her novels, or in the staging of such ideas, Kollontai slips in criticism, especially when members of proletarian society allow the individual to take precedence over the masses. She describes it as a constant tension between one and the others. The future lies in this confrontation. According to Kollontai, then, the point isn't to solve the mystery of love, but rather to experience it in dark wooden cane the doctor had lent me, and the glasses, my body brimming with sharp prostheses. The tension intensified between us. While you desired to destroy me by consummating the act of love, I kissed your wife in the remedy-room, reaching out my hand for syringes pumped with opiates that would eventually fill my dreams with sexualized depictions of your fourth wife's toned legs. I opened her white smock, lifted her skirt, and slipped my tongue between her shaven luxuriances of flesh. I breathed in the scent you breathed. I tasted the same tastes you'd grown accustomed to tasting for the past four years. I'd move her hips with my hands, I'd touch her navel, I'd feel her hard nipples. I seized the golden curls that tumbled over her shoulders and left her neck exposed, biting it violently, feeling her as you'd felt her before.

all its many political dimensions, turning love against the capitalist program. She also tells us that love may be read in its sociological contexts. She describes this in a broad, not terribly interesting way, because she focuses on major power structures, belonging to those who occupy the summits of society and write its history. And you know how untruthful that is. The interesting thing about Kollontai is how she posits fleeting sexual relationships as a benchmark of this development, the problem of property with respect to fidelity and amid the clamor of the struggle between the proletariat and the bourgeoisie. But she also describes these ephemeral relationships as a form of love that neither transforms our will nor engages in nor tarnishes rational work. Love stripped of such acts offers us no wings, she tells us. It neither tires nor consumes, but neither does

Later, I came to you with the taste of her still on my lips, on my hands, between my legs. Maybe you recognized it. Open with incredulity, your mouth revealed to me that I took pleasure in causing you pain and in never allowing your hands to touch my knees, lower my stockings, gently undo the side clasp on my skirt, insert first your fingers into me and then your brand-new penis, penetrating my unshaven flesh. Never letting you pull up my red skirt with your hands or mouth, never letting you undo my leather bra and suck at my breasts until you'd almost swallowed them, never letting you move your body until my legs were completely open as you seized my tongue with your mouth, never letting your saliva invade my mouth or your teeth bite my neck. Never permitting my legs to brush against your newly stitched balls or my liquids to drip onto your chino pants. I found

it move us or catalyze transferences or new means of coexistence. When this collective becomes tangible in the material sphere, only then can it be conceived as a winged Eros: the emotional energy gradually accumulating in these selves seeks to manifest itself in the love-experience. The romantic melodrama that restores everyday development against a backdrop of class tension may be interpreted as a sexual instinct manifested as a seed of plenitude.

You ask me about your interpretation of this text. What can I say, apart from the words I'll invoke from that same book: the collective must be founded through a camaraderie that is contingent on the emotional and intellectual ties connecting its members. The collective is a single tapestry of friendship, passion, maternal touch, infatuation, mutual understanding, more pleasure in denying you such things, particularly the one physical act you most wanted to perform, conscious as you were of your new body. I wouldn't admit, then, that you denied my body's effect on your pen and your intellect, over your spirit and how it shaped materiality. I let you breathe, on me, the scent you found in your bed every night, bored by then of such doctoral discipline. Withholding something from you when you wanted it was equivalent to cutting off your penis, murdering you, and thus transforming you back into a woman and into the object of my affection.

In the dressing room, I was struck by the force gathering in the melodrama, the very same power that, on that opening night, made you approach me with the intent to snatch my fragility away. I walked out onto the stage, barely sympathy and compassion, admiration and familiarity. So why deny oneself a feeling of profound friendship when one feels attracted to or tenderness for someone else? Winged, one experiences both sexual pleasure and the manifestation of love in each everyday element: the creativity that underlies the collective as an idea and an ideal. The point, then, is not to focus on the form taken by love, but rather on mutual acknowledgment, on the creation of a reality that belongs to us in an egalitarian rather than an individual way. A camaraderie-love, then, that recognizes the other's integrity. What is this other than the most intense possible experience of an ethical program? What is sex if not the chance to build another world? What are the wings of this Eros if not what Audre Lorde describes, decades later, in her essay on eroticism as a feminist weapon? Eros isn't only a biological remembering the words I'd so exhaustively rehearsed that they'd become a part of me, the letters imprinted onto the folds of my body. I left the stage, feeling as if I were about to burst, containing the intensity of my emotion through deep breaths that quickly proved useless as the marks emerged, evidence of the blows that my fellow actors had dealt me onstage, hurling me to the ground. Facing the mirror, I saw my face altered by tears and the blood pooling in my cheek. One of the actors apologized, holding out an ice pack to me. I let him place it gently against my cheek and we looked into each other's eyes, though whether we did so as actors or characters, we no longer knew. He stroked my legs, which were dappled with wounds from my fall onto the glass, my ankle re-swelling without its cast. Applause sounded in the background. My scene partner,

force, but also a profoundly social emotion.

You ask about the brother. And I'll tell you: the brother is the sister is the girlfriend. "Despite the immediate recognition that occurs between these bodies, the affective encounter did not transpire until months later, when I wasn't I nor was she he, when we were nothing but curls and tails, furs and wools, softnesses invoking the other's touch. First, we caressed each other with words, we learned our secret names and relished our accents. Then touching on the shoulders and on the arms ensued. Words that invoked our need for the other, an exchange of scents seeping all the way into us. This was followed by the touching of hands, and, trembling, of the face and hair. Then lips and earlobes, until the golden curls that tumbled down over our foreheads had tangled together.

professional, cooled of onstage emotion, eager for recognition, reached out his hand to me and we walked back out to face the audience. Just before we reemerged onstage, I saw the trails of blood I'd left on the floor, the stains you'd tread across in black overshoes like a European hiker. Amid the applause, my feelings dispersed and I inhabited that other place, receiving in my hands your hands and those of my colleague stretching in his dancer's body.

In the daydream, I felt your hands on my wounds. They didn't stop, not grasping whether we were the set design or the performers inhabiting it.

The next day, still in bed, you'd try not to imagine the taut nipples of that actress who was me, shedding a certain shame that would overcome you when you'd

Then came the clasps and embraces. Clothing fell to the ground and the buttons of our breasts appeared, little tits, tails that were penises, milk between the legs, feet that were claws, teeth marks that were scratches and which left gorgeous sketches tattooed across our many-colored coats. That's how we'd suddenly end up: two naked bodies utterly given over to each other, beyond all material circumstances. She was inhabited by her brother, my boyfriend, and his lovers. The animal and spiritual kingdoms appeared, built atop the haze and the brightest clarity. There was nothing but her and me, and that presence was everything, the problem and the solution, the certainty of my individual existence and the impossibility of existing alone. We'd see the past as a wave of the future. Face to face, woven into time and circumstance, we were the everlasting paradox."

stare obsessively at the hard points beneath her blouse, your gaze so piercing that the woman who was me would turn around murmuring when she heard you. The same thing happened that evening as you tended my wounds, kneeling before the woman who was me and was not me.

After the second day of the season, you looked at the lesions from the doorway. My onstage fall and the lead actor's violent outburst had been, more than realistic, real. It was unclear whether the final ovation came from the catharsis prompted by action or by the incontinence of an audience uncomfortable with its own stillness in response to the explosion of violence. With the aid of a magnifying glass and a pair of tweezers, you extracted the shards of glass encrusted from knee to foot in the legs that were sometimes mine.

"What will become of us tomorrow?" you'll ask about the last line in the book. My response can be none other than its echo: "The brother confirms what he already knew, what he'd sensed in the dreams that drenched him at night and seized him by day, the sexual movements of his girlfriends, his sisters, and his mothers. A conversation full of contained emotion transpires between the three of them. Anyone would say that they share a secret language. Desire circulates in endless forms between these three, a desire so carnal that it filters through space and materializes in the bodies of other members of the collective. The conversation lasts for days, weeks, months, perhaps an entire lifetime. The brother finally makes a decision, the one he knew was approaching, given the way of the world. He determines the sacrifice of his masculinity, sphere of

With water and rubbing alcohol, you erased, from the leg that was or wasn't mine, the sketch left by the blood-trails along the skin and its tangled hair. With no other remedies at hand, you placed your cold fingers on the skin that would soon turn mottled purple with the actor's blows. You helped that woman who was and wasn't me to clothe herself in a pair of broad pants, pulled tight around the dancer's leotard that was required of her character, which was also my character. She stood up, wiping off the smears of makeup under her eyes. She applied lipstick and gathered her mane, which had previously tumbled down her back in a flood of curls, at her neck. Together, they went up to celebrate with the rest of the company on the second floor.

After the continuous, thunderous applause, my work was meteoric. A afflictions. Now he will be part of them and he will be made manifest only in the communion between the two. The women weep for days, though they aren't sure if it's because of the brother's sacrifice or because he has passed down his physical and intellectual traits to them, his cathexis and his *petit object-a*, his cracks and his powers for their inhabitation. Now they have to exist with that. They'd never imagined such a world when they stood naked before each other. They mourn the past that was also the future, because they lost what they love most, adding and adding: the sublime brother and the carnal brother. Will it be possible, they'll ask in the future, to bring him back to life and leave him in a museum, say, half alive and half dead, or maybe incorporate him into their own bodies, thus forming a new entity with six legs, six arms, three heads, little tits lining up like a fan?

full year in which you and I fused together in body, intellect, and spirit. Your pen began to change, and you'd inhabit the pages in front of me, on your knees. Mine began to harden and I'd take to the stage, delivering speeches on red love as my golden curls shook fiercely free. Our encounters were many, sporadic, and banal, like you. But we could never ignore the fact that we inhabited each other in every single stroke of our pens.

He said yes because he isn't part of the sacrifice that's been made, but his games delay them for days, months, years. Little by little, they find a way, exchanging parts of their body. But the women soon miss the pleasure they found in their orifices and they despise the murderous impulses triggered by wearing their tails in front. They get used to it. In the end, love becomes absolute in the submission of the brother's and the boyfriend's masculinity, so as to resemble and acquire—half god, half mummy— a coat of golden curls."

You think I don't remember the life we lived together. It was a full year in which you and I fused together in body, intellect, and spirit. We could never ignore the fact that we inhabited each other in every single stroke of our pens. The everlasting lives in us.

When you woke from this brief dream, she was the first image to appear before you.

Her long body stretched out across the cloth, coiled around itself, enveloped in its own blanket, sometimes white, sometimes tiger-print, her eyes half-closed, emitting a piercing light that followed her every movement. He caressed her legs' fleecy coat until her thighs parted. Irises and purring arose. And with them, a soft tail that shuddered when it brushed against her back. He stroked her belly, offered up as it was, and amid the fur he discovered six little teats, lined up in rows, which he explored with his fingers and then with the tip of his tongue. He waited before her, nearly panting now, his lips so wet that they seemed to release a trickle down his chin, swollen with dense hairs that the man would have to shave the next day. He felt the brilliant pelt of her tail curl around his back from the right and slip into his left ear. He imagined her naked. Her furred spots fell, opening like a chrysalis, revealing virgin sunbeam skin, still flecked with a few dark marks of animal hide. She clawed off his shirt. He slowly peeled open her pelt, a little confounded by the foreignness of her body. His own felt foreign, too, invaded by unearthly desire, even when he lay beside the doctor who sometimes shared his bed. He hid his erection and made his way to the bathroom, wiping up traces of viscous liquid from the polished floor of the new house. In the bathroom, their union was absolute. Her golden curls tumbled down her back, and as his tongue, fingers, and member entered into the slick cavities of that body, he lost all grasp of what was ahead and behind, above and below, what he was and what he was not. It was a fleeting, totalizing, and wholly addictive sensation, light, mesmerizing, embodied in that other body that could very well have been someone else with him.

You think I don't remember the life we shared. The closing night we sat at a long table with the rest of the company. In the corner was the actor with the dancer's body, unwaveringly fixated on his psychoanalytic therapy and on flying back to his native British island as soon as possible. Beside him was the girl who was also a boy, whose ambiguity didn't seem to belong to her. She'd squirrel away any hint of intelligence behind her convulsive desire to please. Farther down was the girl with green eyes and black hair, diligent in her inventories and convinced that success meant following instructions. Her life was as planned out as a script. Facing her was the young critic who hovered between the least compelling subjects possible, so fearful of destroying any conversation with her intellect that she'd vanish into wholly superficial matters that didn't actually interest her in the least, beyond serving as a pretext for watching how the others acted and moved about life as if on a stage she could analyze. Beside her was a skeletal woman who gave off the consuming sorrow of someone who still doesn't understand this world and is branded by a confidence that can only be attained with age, experience, and love of life. And beside her, a girl who seemed to be running a thousand-meter race, her voice agitated because she'd given her all in the first hundred, staring with cavernous terror into the future.

I could keep describing what I remember from the night we met again. If I did, I would recall the women seated at the head of the table, two women utterly different from each other, but chameleonic together, each adopting the other as her model, delving into the fascination that one woman can feel for another. Or I could talk about the couple who prevented us from ordering more drinks from the bartender. In the cab, cutting across the city through tunnels and bridges, you asked me about the character who was you in this scene. It's my future, you told me, and the woman writing it was both of us.

Scenes from the
Spectral Zone

Extermination

The Extermination showed up a few weeks before the machines came to Zanjón de la Aguada and drained the swamp (rank, fetid, black). That's what I called him because he didn't scare me like he scared everyone else, and he seemed to like it, or else he just liked that I was nice to him (get away from that filthy thing, you hear me?). I also wasn't scared when I stood at a distance and watched him swallow a frog and then a lizard into the lower half of his body. It actually made me laugh, because that's when I realized the Extermination trailed a little neon path wherever he went, like snails (come on, come look). Which he also ate. He stepped right over them and then they were gone, except for two bright little trails that crisscrossed over each other and a bigger one that kept moving (vrooom). I liked him right away, because I know what it's like to be low-down and not have any friends. Besides, when the Extermination showed up, Remigio was hitting me and everyone else just watched and didn't do anything. The Extermination scared them (every last one, one by one, I told her. And she said: so what did he do to the other kids? 'Cause I sure as hell don't want to fight with the neighbors) and no big kid ever hit me again and I never left the Extermination's side (get over here, you fuckin' brat). We didn't do much that first day. I went up to him and offered him part of a buttered roll my mom had wrapped up for me in a napkin (I'll be home at seven). I took it out of my pocket and the napkin had come off and the butter was smeared all over the place. The Extermination didn't care. He ate it anyway (who knows what kind of shady shit that kid's gotten into). I stuck it into the little hole that opened up in front of me at head-level. I figured it was his mouth because there was a bad smell coming out of it, because he always forgot to brush his teeth (and what about that stench?). Then we sat together on a rock overlooking the river. When night fell, the Extermination gestured to me and disappeared, dragging himself off toward the water (come on, bring your ironing, the telenovela's about to start). The next day, I went looking for him and saw him coming out of the swamp as if it were a cradle. He rose up like a crocodile: first his eyes, then his scaly body, then those gushes of color that seemed to be his clothes (he's hanging out with that crook. He better not go in there or I'll drag him out by his hair). Then I told him I wasn't allowed to swim in the river. He gave me something wrapped up in the same stuff his clothes were made of (nothing but garbage, you know). I went and held it under the faucet. The water started to reveal an orange. We ate it in the middle of the day, when the heat was worst. It tasted good. Remigio showed up at eleven-thirty sharp with Gaby (trashy, stupid, gross) and they started pelting us with green peaches. One smashed me right in the face and I couldn't really see what happened next. But people said later that it was like they'd sprinkled him with water, it slid right off him, and Gaby and Remigio were scared, because the Extermination had sort of stretched himself out long somehow and he looked huge, like he'd hit a growth spurt. (And then he stepped over them and ate them up, just like he'd eaten the snails and the frogs and the lizards. I saw him do it with my own two eyes.)

Then things got weird. People started yelling stuff at us on the street. And since the Extermination started eating other people, the ones who talked, the ones I told him were saying mean things about me and him, they got even more scared (hello, Police, hello, City Hall, hello, Health Services). Meanwhile, the Extermination started to grow, and he grew until he was as big as a house. And people started blaming him for everything (looks like the Extermination nabbed the Gallego, Maribel's husband. I mean, he loved her too much to just walk out, don't you think?). And people started showing up with cameras and they filmed me with the Extermination, and the talking lady covered her nose and mouth with a handkerchief (in this filthy, foul-smelling place, the stench is overpowering. Living conditions are deplorable. Children are dirty and abandoned). Then she threw up, but they left that part out. So I invited the Extermination over to my house so we could watch the nine o'clock news, but my mom wouldn't let him in (get out of here, you revolting thing, don't you dare set foot in my house) and I left with him, because he's my best friend and he eats people to defend me and nobody else ever bothered me or hit me or said anything mean to me again. Then the machines came (toot, toot, toot, vsst, vsst, vsst, vsst) and it was awful, because the Extermination didn't have a place to live or take a bath anymore. We sat on the rock to watch the machines pulling up the mud that had replaced the mucky water that had once been the Extermination's home and they found plastic bottles, little bags of chicken bones, orange peels, cans, clothes, cardboard, a man's skeleton, the top part of a car, some tires, a shovel, some photos, a notebook, a backpack, a piece of plastic from who knows what, cooking pots, an unbroken glass cup and another one made of plastic, a triangular glass, rotten flowers, plates of food, computers, cables, a lamppost, a stuffed panda bear, a petrified tree, an entire armored car, a house, an enormous hole that hurtled forward and shot all the way into the center of the Earth, a pencil, and a pencil sharpener. At least that's what I could see from where we sat. And it rose up like a crazy wind, the steamy haze that had hung around us every day of our lives (finally someone is doing something and let's hope all that garbage goes away, people here don't have anything to eat, kids don't have anywhere to play).

As the days passed and the swamp turned into a construction pit, the Extermination started shrinking and shrinking, until one morning he fit right in the palm of my hand. That's when I thought about giving him a present so he wouldn't feel bad or think people didn't like him. So I got out the blender and stuck in a wooden board, a trash bag, a Coke bottle, some canola oil, a bat, toothpaste, an old engine from a toy car, a little bit of benzene, my mom's hand, and some milk, and I blended it all up. I placed the Extermination on the kitchen floor and poured the mixture onto him. He suddenly started to grow, to feel like himself again. It didn't last long, though. So I had to keep making lots of energy juices like that one, but I was running out of stuff. I didn't have sheets on my bed anymore or underpants or neighbors to help out when they needed it. And I tried to explain it to him with a heavy heart. But I couldn't, because a man showed up in a baseball cap with a logo on it (Why don't you do us all a favor and calm the hell down, young man. You watch yourself now) and blasted us with water from an enormous hose without waiting for an answer. I was soaked. My pants fell down, because I'd given my belt to the Extermination. As I tried to haul them up again so that the new neighbors wouldn't make fun of me, I saw how the Extermination was getting smaller and smaller until his tiny body disappeared, his mole body, his newborn kitten body, his fly body, and his whole self completely dissolved into the water.

The Root

They said there weren't twelve of me when that woman gave birth to us, our arms and our chests and our legs coated in lanugo. The golden beads peeked over the mountains, advancing through the cold valleys of southern Chile. That woman seized us by the dark hair that tangled at our lower backs. She dragged us over hills and valleys until we reached the streambed where the land turned to water. She took the mud and christened us with my name. She sheathed everyone I was in a single word beneath the clay, our skin darkened in the damp. She told us we were one with that earth, it bore her name and she bore mine. Our curls and lanugo grew thickly down to our thighs. We slept on top of them in the fields. We learned to crawl across them. Ensnaring ourselves in them, we learned to follow that woman who wandered barefoot over the carpet of camouflaged leaves. We wore the paint of wet soil ever since we were born to that woman. That's what they told us.

They told us our stories from the other side of the factory gate. Their voices were an Antarctic breeze. It sporadically dispersed the rotten stench impelled by pipes now laid across a streambed that had once belonged to us. The stench, they told us, bore the surname that replaced the root in us. As they muttered in secret, we recalled the first time we ever noticed that rank and penetrating smell. It was when we sprouted our tails:

One cold morning, I was sleeping alone on the hillside, among the bushes, just as that woman had instructed us. Sleep like a log, she'd say, because this land is yours and mine. All I wanted was to obey. A lone man came down the path in a horse-drawn cart. He got out when he saw my twelve bare legs entwined. He wanted to touch them, but he didn't know which. He realized we were having sensual dreams about him and he fled toward the dawn edifice that grew like fungi, drying out everything around it. When we woke, we saw that a smooth, furry tail had sprouted from the base of our spines. It stirred up dust and took on the color of the earth when it rustled against our curls. Our legs smelled of man and our twelve noses pricked at the whiff of industrial plague. Its smokes and waters rose artificially up the hills.

Their voices soft, their lips drawn close to my twelve pairs of ears, they reminded me what we did next. I took off my clothes by the streambed. Springy-tailed, I splashed earthy water onto my skin. That, they told us, was how they saw us for the first time. Our lanugo stood on end when we felt the Antarctic wind, the strong man-smell that accompanied their rhythmic voices. Our twelve pairs of eyes fixed the new arrivals with terror. I'd never seen anything like those creatures with their furry tails in front. They reminded us that they'd gotten into the water and the mud with us. They too had washed themselves of the pungent reek that had so abruptly pervaded the valley and the hills.

Their voices like breath, they told us how our twelve lips had joined their own and that our backs fused together in an obscene embrace. That our twelve pairs of sun-browned arms intermingled with legs as thick and long as sprigs of wheat. I unfurled my twelve tails to touch the neck of one of the new arrivals, seeping into their ears with talk that soon grew intimate. In the grit stirred up by all this anarchy, my curls inserted themselves into their earthy caverns until I lost count of how many bodies we were, how many words contained us.

Inside the gate, we looked at each other and tried using our words to remember what had happened:

At night, my twelve tails writhed at the sensual memory of all the men now crossing the valleys and the hills. We walked through where the boldo forests shifted into pine and damp, into desert and dust. Our twelve pairs of power and tails slipped away in the sun, dulling our skins that startled at the smell of the factory, repulsive as a magnet.

Their voices unfettered on the other side of the gate, they told us we'd been crawling around the entrance when the factory guards spotted us there. The uniformed men crossed themselves at the sight of our bushy bodies, our dirty hides, our lush tails, our plugged snouts. Before their insensitive muzzles, in their mechanical eaglet eyes, in their mouths full of illogical promises, I was the very vision of human misery.

Whispering, they told us that men in white appeared with the same name sewn onto their hearts: Laroote Matte Paper Mill. With their voices dark in the murky night, they reminded us what that woman had said: despair will come from white. But we didn't remember. Our memory had moved away from us when their touch petrified our tails. Through the guards' peephole, the men in white suits, white aprons, white togas with their hearts stitched in Ls, As, Rs, Os, Ts, Es, Ms, and Ss offered me combs and silver beads to decorate my tail with. All twelve of us crossed through the gate.

Their voices sullen, they told us that the men in white had put us in a swimming pool with chlorinated water. White were their words recited from a book of white pages. White was the god who wished to donate his patronymic to us so that we would no longer be one. They sloshed us with water and scrubbed us down. They plunged our heads underwater to christen us with the name. They called us: María de las Trinidades Jesús de la Concepción Consuelo Magdalena José. Our lanugo fell out and our tails fell off. The channels swept our fur toward the river and then out to sea, along with the rest of the factory waste. And they stitched our hearts with the same surname as everyone else's. We were Javieras Fernandas Renatas Rosas Encomenderos Gutiérrez de los Laroote Matte. Now we, all twelve of us females, were the factory, they told us, and we'd become one with the white doctors, the white priests, and the white workers who had arrived to construct the building, which was also white. But we were also the females who were supposed to make paper by threading the fibers of the trees where that woman had given birth to us. Little by little, our skins dulled, our hairs lightened, and we started forgetting about the root.

The moon barely illuminated the faces of our interlocutors. Not even twelve pairs of eyes could make out their blue bodies on the other side of the white gate. They asked us if we remembered our name. I answered for all of us: María Martirio de la Eterna Concepción, number twenty ninety fifty-five and six. They inquired, touching their long fingers to our twelve white uniforms, if we knew who had conceived us. We told them what was said in the factory aisles: that our parents lived in Santiago de los Chiles, but they'd be visiting us soon to pet and school us.

With their voices, they told us the news from beyond the gate: rumor had it that the Laroote Mattes appeared one day at dusk and were staying in a house by the ocean. When they looked out the window, they might very well see the dark stain on the river's mouth, the mixture of the factory waste and our lanugo.

And in their conspiratorial whispers, they confessed to us: we're looking for that woman. And with the caresses their tentacles lavished on our hair, now lighter in color and gathered into a bun, they asked: do you know what's become of her? And as they loosed our hair from its tie, letting our curls tumble down over our white apron, their muted voices asked about that woman's body. They threatened us with every touch: your secret hair will grow and twelve tails will make you remember.

We let ourselves be loved that night as we'd done once on the muddy riverbank. But a couple of our eyes saw that their hands held notebooks to write down our secret name.

For days, we allowed their muted voices to tell us our stories, allowed their course hands to coax our black lanugo into growth. At dawn, we'd comb each other's long curls and thick-haired spots, which were starting to appear on the short tails we now had between our legs. And we remembered:

We dug a hole in the material made with ground *canelo* wood all the way down to where the rank green earth appeared with its boldo fluff. We kept digging until we found the very first bone that had belonged to that woman. We dug deeper and deeper in search of the second bone, then the third, then the twentieth, then the hundred seventy-fifth, until we collected two hundred six bones altogether. Up on land, we promised her a burial.

We emerged from the ground. We appeared on the barren, fetid plots that housed the Larootes and the Mattes, our parents, in bedrooms with sealed windows. From the roofs, we could see them sleeping on the lanugo lost to years and years of obscurity. With our long tails, we inserted sensual dreams into their bodies, which were covered in our color of hair. They jolted awake, terrified, splashing themselves with water from the depths of the earth, which sprouted up as black as when the ground was ours. It dirtied their hair and the mud stripped them of our lanugo, which they'd planted on their skins with the secret name that belonged to us.

The twelve of me sprouted into a hundred. Once there were a hundred of me, we became legion. With the power of the breeze from our lips, we blew the progenitors of oblivion right from their beds. We yanked their mattresses out from under them, we jerked the bristles from their beards and their backs, we wrested away our skins. And we took the curls, which were our curls. We dragged heaps of them over the hills and valleys until we reached the streambed where the land turned to water. We buried that woman's bones in the mud, we buried that lanugo from which I was born, and we sheathed the name that marked the earth and me in water and earth.

Then the storm hit and made the land grow wild with roots. Wherever the men in white aprons happened to be, they would see lanugo burgeoning between the concrete and the industrial mushrooms, and they would hear the secret name spoken loud and clear: the name that hails from all our fragrant winds, our own damp earth.

Instructions for the Eye

Our voice sounds at the first light in twenty centuries of affliction: we envision the entrance to the exhibition space as a glass pane with nothing attached to it, not even a handle. It would open at the merest touch of a hand or the nearby presence of a body at room temperature. Entirely transparent, lacking any fixture for the hand to clutch, passers-by would continually bump into it as it swung open.

Our narration sounds better than the Champs-Élysées: we'd glimpse a gallery-goer, hopefully the artist herself, walk right into the glass and gash her eyebrow, leaving a permanent scar. We'd notice a line of blood trickling into her eye.

Our voices sound like anesthesia: eventually the swelling and dried blood would make it impossible for her to actually see the exhibition space. We'd also strip the artist of her capacity to make out the people milling around the gallery, looking at her art or entering through the glass doors.

Our narration sounds like silk threads stitching skin: no one in the massive audience would recognize the woman with the swollen, bloody eye as the creator of the works on display.

Our voices sound like the subway screeching: we'd notice a half-blind older woman with bluish hair and tremblingly painted eyebrows who'd squint her eyes, clutch the artist's arm, and ask her to narrate what she saw.

Our voices sound like tradition: we envision the exhibition space as a plane painted on the ceiling, hopefully onto a mirror or some lighter reflective material. The plane would indicate the kinds of movement and specific actions with which the viewers should approach the works. Occasionally, we would see the visitors twist their necks to regard their own bodies at unusual angles.

The narration sounds like a multitude: we'd see the artist, who is also hard of hearing, leading the old woman into the adjacent room, inventing how the works should be heard. We follow her with our eyes.

Our voices sound like solace: there would be markings on the floor to instruct the observers how to position themselves before the works of art. Never in a fixed position, always in motion, always at an uncomfortable angle for the eyes. Solid bodies would impede them from looking.

Our voices break the glass and smash the cornets: the first piece would be made of a shaft of light emerging from the floor and aiming at the roof. Laser-like, it would give the impression of piercing the bodies it illuminates. If a viewer were to stare directly into the beam, it would blind her.

Our narration is diluted by the wind: ideally, a passing body would activate a camera and a flash.

Our voices have no origin: one of the people photographed would have a swollen eye.

Our narration sounds like a distant continent: when the flash went off, the old woman would clutch the arm of the artist with the scab over her eye, marking her skin with her enameled nails.

The voice rises up from the afterlife: beside the artist with the bruised and blood-caked eye and the old woman with blue hair, we'd observe a woman doing a performance and announcing the artist's name into the microphone. Nobody would know where to look.

Our voice multiplies eternity: we'd notice tiny metal balls scattered all over the floor that would occasionally deprive bodies of stability as they stopped to observe the art. We'd offer alcohol to their organisms so that they feel they've lost their way entirely.

Our narratives resound in several cities: observed from up close, the little metal balls would clearly reveal themselves as elongated, eye-like objects. More than one person would stuff some into their pockets.

We look like solitary animals as we narrate: we would try to keep the little metal balls from straying beyond the hall and rolling across the dribbles of blood that would streak the gallery floor after trickling down from an artistic eye.

Our narration sounds like a cap and gun: one of the pieces, a wax doll, would imitate the security guards. The doll would wear a black suit, pants, vest, and jacket. Its shirt would be white and a delicate tie would cut across its torso. It would be wearing pale blue shoes. The doll made to represent a male or female guard would have an intercom at its ear and its hand would conceal a diminutive notebook that, if moved, would allow it to take notes on the viewers it monitored.

A voice rings out: the doll that represents a male or female guard would have a liquid eye. This would be barely perceptible. Someone in the crowd would take a long, prudent while to realize that the person monitoring them was not in fact a person but just a doll. To do so, she would have to look the doll directly in the eye. Its texture would disappear with any change in the angle of observation.

The narration seeks half-tones: visitors would reach a wall where what looks like a painting is hung, but which is actually a 1.3 by 2.8-meter low-thickness Plexiglas block. The surface would be marked to imitate patches of lawn. The drawings would suggest the blueprint of a garden. But it would be indiscernible to the naked eye. To make it visible, one would have to fix it with a light source, which means that all we'd see would be the shadow of the lines on the Plexiglas.

Our narrative grows raucous: in the adjacent hall, the floor would be scattered with ears. Ideally, the bodiless organs would be located in the garden, in the middle of nature, in such a way that the pieces are clearly the remnants of a massacre.

Our voice will never go silent: in the middle of the hall of ears, there would be a glass box with a handwritten book and a series of drawings and seals. Some of them would say: "popular tragedy," "smoking in the sun," "landing as a group," "dressing up in costume and going out," "distant mirror." They would be printed on wood, cork, or plastic with fluorescent ink and a seal of a wine glass or a loaf of bread between the words. At the end, it would say "In Memoriam, Édouard Levé."

We read from the book in a weary voice: it would say that a tongue cleans the broken eye in its studio. There's a typewriter hammering away at the instructions for the eye. With each click-clack, a text is fashioned out of prostheses: fake legs, corsets bound to a lover's back, a cast sheathing a great-aunt, a drunk tongue on a false eye, the paper tongue fluttering at a gold tooth, a hand sketching shapes on a misty pane of glass, a wig on the shelf.

Our voices echo like dismembered animals: the artist would thus envision a space with different human body parts suspended in a metal ring.

Our narration is also a mantra: there are people who would travel to the gallery like participants in a religious procession.

Our voices fade into silence: there would be a mirror in the middle of the room. The old blue-haired woman and the artist would make their way toward it.

The narration fuses into the ambient noise: as people walk along, the origin of every human species would be explained. Pages and pages of bodies would pass by. It would all look like the inside of a subway car, paneled with posters telling the story of humanity like an endangered animal.

The narration is confused with the people following the artist and the old blue-haired woman: the mirror wouldn't reflect the entire image, just what the observer could see. In this way, neither the old blue-haired woman nor the artist with the swollen eye would see her own reflection. They would only hear the tales told by the visitors to describe their actions, as if they too were part of the exhibition.

Notes

"Dead Men Don't Rape" first appeared in *Tupelo Quarterly*. An excerpt from "Cars on Fire" was published in *Anomaly*.

Cars on Fire contains quotes by many other writers and artists, including Marosa di Giorgio, Gabriela Mistral, Sigmund Freud, Jacques Lacan, Cathy Caruth, Julia Kristeva, Édouard Levé, Ernst Jünger, Lourdes Casal, Audre Lorde, Alexandra Kollontai, Ovid, 7 Year Bitch, a message from immaterial beings, and several speeches by former presidents whose names we would do well to forget.

MÓNICA RAMÓN RÍOS was born in Santiago de Chile. She is the author of the novel *Segundos* (2010) and the twin novels *Alias el Rucio* and *Alias el Rocío* (2014-2015). As a scholar, she has written extensively on Latin American literature and film. Her short stories have appeared in several anthologies and journals such as *Anomaly*, *Granta* [Spain], *Asymptote*, *Alba*, and *Buensalvaje*. Ríos is also one of the creators of Sangría Editora, a publishing collective based in Santiago and New York.

ROBIN MYERS was born in New York and is based in Mexico City. She is the author of several collections of poetry published as bilingual editions in Mexico, Argentina, and Spain. Her translations have appeared in *Asymptote*, the *Los Angeles Review of Books*, *Waxwing*, *Inventory*, and elsewhere. Her translation of Ezequiel Zaidenwerg's *Lyric Poetry Is Dead* was published by Cardboard House Press in 2018.

OPEN LETTER

WWW.OPENLETTERBOOKS.ORG

**OPEN
LETTER**